THE BATTLE OF JUNK MOUNTAIN

Lauren Abbey Greenberg

RP|KIDS
PHILADELPHIA

Running Press Kids
Hachette Book Group
1290 Avenue of the Americas, New York, NY 10104
www.runningpress.com/rpkids
@RP_Kids

Printed in the United States of America

First Edition: April 2018

Published by Running Press Kids, an imprint of Perseus Books, LLC,
a subsidiary of Hachette Book Group, Inc.
The Running Press Kids name and logo is a trademark of the Hachette Book Group.

The Hachette Speakers Bureau provides a wide range of authors for speaking events. To find out more, go to www.hachettespeakersbureau.com or call (866) 376-6591.

The publisher is not responsible for websites (or their content) that are not owned by the publisher.

Print book cover and interior design by T. L. Bonaddio.

Library of Congress Control Number: 2017947054

ISBNs: 978-0-7624-6295-7 (hardcover), 978-0-7624-6296-4 (ebook)

LSC-C

10 9 8 7 6 5 4 3 2 1

FOR MY TREASURES:
Brian, Jacob, and Ellie

CHAPTER 1

THIS IS MY HAPPY PLACE

I didn't expect my summer sister to ditch me the first minute of vacation. She could've at least waited until I emptied my suitcase.

"But . . . but . . ." I sputter like the last seconds of microwave popcorn. "What about going to Lolli's?"

Poppy sighs. "I'm sorry. I wish I could, but the last time I didn't show up for a shift, my dad totally freaked out."

I sink onto what will be my bed for the next month. "But we always go to Lolli's for milkshakes first thing. It's tradition."

"It sucks, I know, but . . ." She shrugs. "Our tradition will have to change."

Change? What's she talking about? The best thing about Thomas Cove is that nothing ever changes.

I stare at the stack of neatly folded T-shirts on my lap. "Couldn't your dad wait for you to start working at the store until you're older? Nobody I know back home works full-time when they're twelve."

She sits next to me cross-legged and examines the bottoms of her bare feet. "It's different here. Kids start hauling lobster traps by the time they're eight years old. Consider me lucky."

Poppy's parents own Quayle's Market, the only grocery store on Cedar Island. Her two older sisters have worked there for years. I guess it was only a matter of time before she got roped in. But why did it have to be *this* summer, the first one without my parents?

Sunlight streams through the window, making Poppy's auburn hair glow like a maple tree in fall. "You could come with me. I have to stock the shelves and stuff, and it's kind of boring, but at least it's not the fish counter."

"Thanks, but I guess I should stay here. I'm ready to get this project going, if you know what I mean." I tug on the top drawer of the pine dresser in an attempt to put my clothes away, but it's stuck shut. The one under it opens easily, but it's full of miniature glass ducks, piles of old comic books, and several cat calendars. Looks like my grandmother's been trolling the yard sales . . . again.

My cheeks puff out. This is going to be a bigger job than I thought.

I catch my reflection in the cracked floor-length mirror. The damp Maine air has wreaked havoc on my curly hair already. I pat down the puffed-out ponytail at the base of my neck. Ugh, I look like a beaver.

Poppy rolls onto her stomach, smooshing the ruffled blue throw pillows beneath her. Together we peer out the window. The view outside is postcard pretty, the kind parents pay top dollar for at a hotel. A lobster boat cuts through the water; its motor drones steadily as it passes anchored skiffs that rock gently back and forth in its wake. Next door to us, a hulk of a man wearing a camouflage baseball cap chops firewood. Sweat darkens the back of his dingy gray tank.

"Is that the new neighbor?" I ask.

"Yup, that's Cranky."

"Cranky?"

"His real name is Mr. Holbrook, but I call him Cranky, because that's what he is. Every time I see him, he has this look on his face like he just bit into a vomit burger. He's so mean, Shayne. He'll yell at you if you cut through his yard. You can't use his dock—"

I gasp. "No dock jumping?"

"Nope. All his property is off-limits."

Drat. The old neighbors, the Krafts, used to let us have full run of their place like it was our own private playground.

"When he moved in, my mom made me bring over a plate of cookies. As soon as I stepped into his yard, he appeared from

3

behind a tree, clutching a great big ax, his eyes wild and crazy. I screamed and took off, dropped the cookies and everything. He started yelling at me, and his voice was so gravelly, like he ate pebbles for breakfast."

"Hold on. Important question. What kind of cookies were they?"

"White chocolate chunk."

I press my hand over my heart. "Tragic waste."

"You know what else?" Poppy lowers her voice. "Mona said that when he moved in, there was no moving truck, nothing. He has no furniture and he sleeps alone on the bare wood floor with nothing but a hunting knife beside him."

Goose bumps cover my arms, even though I'm not sure if I should believe her. Poppy always says that her sister is a big fat liar.

I reach for the tin box where I keep all my supplies for making friendship bracelets. Last year, Poppy and I cranked them out like crazy, and I'm happy to see she still has the blue-and-green one I made her wrapped around her wrist.

"I brought a whole bunch of colors," I say, showing her my new pack of embroidery thread.

"Oooh, I like the neon green," she says before twitching her nose. "No offense, but you need to air out this room. It smells like old people."

I open the window, and the scents of salt, fish, and pine needles blow in at once. "Don't worry. When I'm through with this place, you won't even recognize it."

"I can't believe your mom's making you clean up your grandmother's house," she says.

"She didn't make me. I offered to come. Anyhow, it's not so much about cleaning up as getting her ready to sell her stuff at the Cedar Island Flea Market."

I place my bracelet tin on top of a tower of *National Geographic* magazines so old and worn they've practically molded into a small table.

Poppy glances at her watch, then hops off the bed. "I better go. Don't want the boss to ground me." She rolls her eyes.

I walk her down the stairs to the front door. Wooden signs of various shapes and sizes decorate the walls, some with beach themes (LIFE IS BETTER IN FLIP-FLOPS), some spouting puns (GARDENERS KNOW ALL THE DIRT), and others offering warm fuzzies (THIS IS MY HAPPY PLACE).

Poppy shouts over the sound of a blaring TV. "Bye, Bea!"

Everyone calls my grandmother by her first name. Even me.

"Bye, Poppy!" Bea yells from the family room.

Poppy squeezes my shoulders and gives me a friendly shake before she leaves. "Don't worry. We still can have the Best. Summer. Ever. You'll see."

Doubt prickles my skin. The best summer ever means morning swims in the cove, searching for sea glass, riding bikes to Lolli's, gorging on lobster rolls—stuff we've been doing for years. Now she's *sort of* available. What am I supposed to do when she's sort of not?

CHAPTER 2

MY HOUSE WAS CLEAN LAST WEEK ... SORRY YOU MISSED IT

After Poppy leaves, I join Bea in the family room. She sits at what I like to call Junk Mountain, the epicenter of all her worldly possessions. When it comes to stuff, my grandmother's a keeper. She keeps everything.

Everything.

Some kind of table supports Junk Mountain, but I have no idea what it looks like because it has always been buried under an avalanche of old books, cracked dishes, stuffed Beanie Babies, and a gazillion other things. A mothball smell hovers like a rain cloud over the pile.

Whenever we visit, my parents note that Junk Mountain has expanded in height and width, and my mother practically breaks out in hives at the sight of it. You would never guess she and Bea were related. Mom calls my grandmother names behind her back like "pack rat," "Dumpster diver," and "eBay explosion." But Bea sees it differently. She calls herself a "collector of everything."

"Sit with me. I need to talk to you." Bea writes a number on a piece of masking tape and sticks it to the bottom of a pumpkin candle.

I turn down the volume on the TV and pull up a folding chair beside her. A furry key chain dyed grapey purple catches my eye. "Is this a real rabbit's foot?" When I touch the bottom, I feel pointy toenails.

Bea examines it. "I'm not sure, although, they say if it's real, then it's good luck." She passes me a shoebox with the words GOOD LUCK written in her shaky scrawl. "Here, add it to the rest of my charms."

I sift through a jumble of dream catchers, four-leaf clover pins, and tiny Buddha figurines. "So, how long do we have to get ready for the flea market?"

"One week," she says.

My eyes grow wide. I hadn't realized it was so soon. "And all this needs to be sorted and priced, right?"

She waves her hands over the merchandise. "So many memories, my treasures. Not only do I remember where I found each item, but I could tell you how much I paid for it and who I was with."

Please, don't.

I inch my chair closer and pull a yellowed teacup from the mound. "This looks ancient. How much should we sell it for?"

"Ah, ah, gentle." She removes it from my hand and inspects it through the wire-rimmed glasses perched on the end of her nose. "Mark that as twenty-five cents."

I frown. "What, only a quarter? I thought it was special."

She hands me a Sharpie. "It *is* special. This teacup may not look like much, but it represents history, memories. It's—" Her brown eyes enlarge. "Now, what's this doing here?" She reaches for a beak poking out from under a cowboy hat and pulls out a silver bird statue.

"Nice chicken," I say.

Her forehead creases. "It's a pheasant. Look at this work-manship, the detail in the feathers."

I stifle a yawn. "Mmm-hmm."

"Your grandpa gave it to me years ago when I was in my bird phase. I remember he paid a couple hundred dollars for it. I could have killed him. We didn't have that kind of money to spare. But I did some research and found out it was made by a famous Russian artist. I believe it's worth *a lot*. Do me a favor, dear, put this on the mantel. It's not for sale. Not yet, anyway."

I set it down over the fireplace, next to my favorite picture of Grandpa. He squints at the camera from the helm of his lobster boat. His face is sunbaked and lined like an alligator's skin. I really miss him.

I dust off my hands on the back of my white shorts. "So . . . is that what you wanted to talk to me about?"

Her face falls. "Well, not exactly. I have some news." She stands and I notice a black apron stamped with a fish print tied around her waist. "Surprise," she says, sounding as excited as if it were Meatloaf Monday. "I went back to work."

"What? I thought you retired years ago."

Bea retrieves a tube of lipstick out of her apron pocket and paints her thin lips bright pink. "The truth is when Grandpa died, he didn't leave me with much. You would be surprised how much everything costs—the house, utilities, you know, other stuff."

I eye the buried table, the couch strewn with magazines and newspapers, the kitchen counter littered with boxes and cans. Yeah, I know "stuff."

Bea coughs into her fist and catches a glimpse of her watch. "Darn it, I'm late."

I follow her to the kitchen. "You're leaving *now*?"

She grabs her enormous sack of a purse off the counter. "I'm sorry, horrible timing, but it's just the lunch shift. I'll be back in a jiffy."

First Poppy's news and now this. *Are you kidding me?* I cross my arms in a huff. "Aren't you too old to be a waitress?"

"I beg your pardon." Bea tries to swat me with a dish towel, and I jump out of the way. "I've waitressed for more than thirty years. Of course, I was nervous at first, going back and all, but then I had forgotten how much I missed the Cod Café."

Aside from a few roadside takeout shacks, the Cod Café is the only full-service restaurant on the island, known for its enormous lobster platters and famous potato salad tossed in Secret Sauce. The servers are usually college kids from the mainland. I want to remind Bea of this, but from the insulted look on her face, I know I have said enough.

Bea finds a leftover tuna sandwich in the fridge and takes two nibbles before putting it back. "Do me a favor, don't tell your mother." She grabs an industrial-sized can of hairspray from her purse and fumigates her frosted mass of curls along with the entire room.

I cough. "How come?"

Bea sighs like she's already answered this question a thousand times. "Let's just say she gets . . . funny about money."

Her pace quickens, and I follow her to her beat-up Subaru wagon.

"Wait, what about our project?" I motion behind me. "I can't tackle that all by myself."

She reaches for the door handle but pauses before turning to me. "You don't need to touch a thing. We'll sort through my treasures later this afternoon, okay?"

The slam of the door makes quick tears sting the back of my eyeballs. Why is everyone leaving me?

She drives away. A hush falls over the cove except for the occasional tinkling of a distant wind chime. The windswept grass tickles my calves as I cut across Bea's yard. A thick rock wall separates her lawn from the sea, and the still water has a copper color to it, like an old penny. Maybe I'll jump in and swim five hundred miles home to Maryland. I'll say to my mom, "I couldn't do it. I failed."

Ha! Never.

CHAPTER 3

PUT YOUR BIG GIRL PANTS ON AND DEAL WITH IT

With a few hours to kill, I skip down the aluminum ramp that connects Bea's backyard to a floating wooden dock. A small white boat, securely moored to a thick post, bobs under my weight as I climb aboard. Bea's fishing skiff is called *Knot for Sale*. Grandpa came up with the name. It was his way of teasing Bea about her yard sale and flea market obsessions.

Seated at the bow, I remove a tangle of embroidery floss from my front pocket and choose cornflower blue and battleship gray threads, colors that match my current mood. Even though a lot of my friends are "over" making friendship bracelets, it's still one of my all-time favorite things to do. The repetition of weaving and knotting kind of puts me in a trance, especially when I need to sort things out in my head.

I think about my friends back home. Zoe and Maya went to some sleepaway camp in West Virginia. Mom had tried to sell me on the idea.

"What about Maine?" I countered. That started a whole fight. Mom told me that this year my dad had to fly to Egypt for a documentary film he's producing, and she was slammed with work from her real estate business. It was like they'd totally forgotten that we go to Maine every August. My begging and pleading pretty much went ignored, but then Bea saved the day. She happened to call a few days later and told my mom she needed to sell some of her things at the Cedar Island Flea Market this summer. That's when the brilliant idea came to me. I reminded Mom about all the community service hours I had earned collecting, sorting, and selling books for the Monroe High School used-book sale. Sometimes I still catch a phantom whiff of musty pages on my fingers. Helping out Bea couldn't be that different, right? Eventually, Mom agreed. She probably just wanted me out of her hair so she could show houses morning, noon, and night without feeling guilty about it, but I figure that's a win for everyone.

To be fair, I had an ulterior motive. I couldn't imagine a summer without seeing Poppy, who lives on the opposite side of the cove from Bea. We had our first playdate when we were like three years old, and I've spent every August with her since. The funny thing is, we're so different that you wouldn't even think we'd be friends. She's loud, I'm soft. I like mustard, she's ketchup only. Poppy's convinced she could be a reality TV star.

I hate those kinds of shows. But we both like lazy summers, making bracelets, and collecting sea glass, and two years ago at my grandpa's funeral, she was the one who held my hand the whole time and passed me tissues when the tears wouldn't stop.

With a loud sigh, my eyes wander to where the mouth of the cove feeds into Casco Bay. A long-ago memory of my grandpa bubbles to the surface. He's in his lobster boat, heading out to check on his traps. His bright orange fishing waders pop against a backdrop of misty gray skies. I'm standing on the dock with my mom, watching him. The motor gurgles as he pulls away, and I can hear Mom saying, "Wave bye-bye to Grandpa." I do, but then out of nowhere, thick fog rolls in and he completely disappears. It totally freaks me out, like some wet, white monster swallowed him whole. I scream and cry while my mother tries to calm me down. Then the sound of a bullhorn pierces the air. Grandpa must have heard me carrying on, so he blew the horn to tell me that everything was all right. And it was . . . that time.

I'm so lost in the memory that I have completely spaced on the bracelet. I must have missed a knot or something, because the pattern's not even. Drat. I have to start over.

As I hoist myself out of the boat, I hear loud rock music in the distance. A couple of shirtless guys in a speedboat careen into the cove like it's the Indy 500. They're not supposed to be going that fast, and I feel like yelling *Slow down!* but someone beats me to it.

I hurry up the ramp to find Cranky screaming at the boys. Standing on his dock, he shakes his fist high in the air. I have to admit, I wouldn't want to cross him. He's pretty big and beefy for an old guy. The boys couldn't care less, though. They drive their boat in a circle, creating a huge, obnoxious wake.

Suddenly, Cranky twists as if he senses me. I duck behind a thicket of rosebushes as my heart hammers my rib cage.

The sound of tires crunching over gravel makes me realize he's not interested in me. A dark gray minivan pulls into Cranky's driveway. The first thing I notice is the magnet on the back of the van that says I HEART HISTORY.

A man with a scraggly beard steps out of the car. He looks as if he marched off a Civil War battlefield with his navy cap, black boots, and wool coat belted with a wide buckle. To be honest, the way he's dressed isn't all that surprising. All kinds of, let's say, *unique* people reside on Cedar Island. There's the man who travels around town on his riding mower, and the lady who wears a floral crown in her hair every day, even when it rains. What's interesting, though, is the way Cranky's looking at this costumed visitor: with disgust. He doesn't say *Hello* or *Can I help you?* or *Do you need directions?* Which is not very Cedar Island–ish at all. I can't make out what they're saying, but there's a lot of angry faces and finger pointing as the two men walk toward Cranky's weathered, gray house. I'm so confused. This is the worst welcome wagon ever.

A boy who looks to be my age hops out of the van. He's wearing a scaled-down version of Beardy's soldier outfit—same cap and boots, but instead of the coat, his white billowy shirt is untucked and rumpled. He glances at the house, then wanders in the direction of my hideout. The boy sits on the other side of the rosebush, only a few feet away from me. Trying hard not to breathe, I carefully push aside a couple branches, making the red, cherrylike flowers bounce up and down.

The boy takes a swig from the old-fashioned canteen slung over his shoulder. I lean my face further into the foliage to spy on him.

Owwww!

Hot pain radiates from the center of my left cheek. Clutching my face, I stumble out from behind the bush.

"Are you okay?" The boy hovers over me. He smells kind of ripe, like maybe it's not a good idea to wear long sleeves and tall boots on a hot day.

I curl into a ball. "I think something bit me."

"Can I see?" His light eyebrows push together with concern as I remove my hand. "The stinger's in there," he says. In one quick motion, he brushes a fingernail against my cheek. "It's out."

I sit up and pat the tender spot. "It is?"

"Linc, get in here, your father needs you." Up on his sagging porch, with hands on hips, Cranky looks, well . . . cranky.

"Coming, Grandpa," the boy says.

Before I can even thank him, he runs into the house and slams the screen door.

CHAPTER 4

LOON SANCTUARY—KEEP OUT

I go to bed early that night, eager to put this weird day behind me and push the reset button. Besides, mornings on Thomas Cove are the best: waking up to beautiful scenery, the sounds of seabirds, and, if I'm lucky, the smell of blueberry muffins baking in the oven.

No such luck. Instead, the telephone's shrill ring bolts me from a deep sleep. I squint—the sheer curtains do nothing to block the rising sun. The digital clock's glowing red numbers confirm my worst fears—it's six o'clock in the morning.

I rub the crusts from the corners of my eyes and drag myself into the bathroom I share with Bea. Ugh, my cheek. It's not super swollen, but it's puffy enough to look like a ginormous mosquito bite. Great.

I open the mirrored cabinet, wondering if I should put something on it. All of Bea's old-people products pack the shelves, tubes of this and jars of that. Some pills spill out from tipped bottles with caps that haven't been put on right. I feel like I'm seeing something I shouldn't.

Muffled sounds seep from under Bea's closed bedroom door. Pressing an ear against the wood, I can hear her talking on the phone. Her clipped words and strained voice give it away, not to mention only one person on earth would call this early in the morning: Mom.

"I was going to tell you . . . I've been busy . . ." Bea says. "She's fine . . . You didn't have to do that . . . Stop worrying . . ."

This is my fault. I wish I hadn't called my mom yesterday like a crybaby, but I couldn't help it. First ditched, then stung, I had to talk to *someone*. Then, without meaning to, I blurted Bea's secret about going back to work. I have an urge to barge in and interrupt the call, but Bea has a thing about her bedroom. She calls it her private sanctuary and never lets anyone in. To drive the point home, a thin aluminum sign hangs from the door that says LOON SANCTUARY KEEP OUT. (Even though a loon is an aquatic bird, my mother would beg to differ.)

The stairs creak as I head to the kitchen to find breakfast. A bowl of cinnamon oat cereal seems to be the only option. My vision of eating in front of the TV is quickly dashed—Bea's dark green plush couch, which was halfway clean yesterday, is now covered with piles of random stuff. I lean against the wall and wonder what this new day holds for me. I have no freaking idea.

A soft clinking noise draws me to the window. Under an electric sky of pink and orange streaks, that boy from yesterday—Linc, I guess—is already outside, setting up what looks like some kind of canvas tent. Wild theories pop into my mind. Maybe Cranky never invited him in the first place, so he kicked him out, making him sleep in the yard with the chipmunks. Linc was probably so excited to see his long-lost grandfather, but Cranky couldn't care less. Wow, what a jerk.

Bea enters the room in her pale blue nightgown, her lips pressed together in an irritated mash. She hands me the phone before heading to the kitchen.

"Hi, Mom."

"You sound tired," she says.

"I just woke up. In normal-people land, this is really early."

A keyboard clicks on the other end of the line. "I wouldn't know. I've been up for hours working."

Mom recently left the real estate company she was with for fifteen years to strike out on her own. It's great that she gets to be her own boss, but it also turned her into a sleepless, stressed-out pain in the butt, so it kind of sucks for the rest of us.

"I've been doing a lot of thinking since our call yesterday," she says, slurping what's probably her third cup of coffee. "Bea put me in a weird spot. I had no idea that you'd be unsupervised for most of the day."

"Mom, I'm not a baby. It's no big deal," I say with a mouth full of cereal.

"You're not a baby, but what if something happens while she's gone? You told me yourself that Poppy's not around as much. The thought of you cooped up alone in that house— don't even tell me what condition it's in; I don't want to know. I've been having nightmares about mold spores."

I remove the phone from my ear, all slack-mouthed. While her *wah-wah-wahs* float into the air, I tackle the messy couch. I can't help it—I love to organize stuff. I take all the scattered DVDs (why Bea has five copies of *Toy Story 3*, I'll never know) and stack them next to the box of record albums stored underneath Junk Mountain. The plastic Easter eggs go to the holiday pile, the old tennis racket goes with the sports stuff, and these leopard ballet slippers . . . how about I start a new pile called Unknown.

There, just enough space to stretch my legs. When I rejoin the conversation, Mom is still going strong.

". . . I've known Ray for years and he said it's okay."

"Said what's okay?"

She huffs. "Shayne, have you been listening at all? The manager at the Cod Café said you could work there during Bea's shifts."

My shoulders tighten. "Work? Why do I have to work? I'm old enough to stay by myself. Nothing will happen, I promise."

"It's not you I'm worried about, honey, it's . . ." She pauses. "I'd feel better if I knew you had a place to go to every day. Think of it like camp."

"Without the fun part," I add.

Her voice softens. "Could you do this for me? I've got one chronically indecisive client, paperwork up to my eyeballs, and Dad just informed me that filming will probably last four weeks instead of three. You said you wanted to help Bea. Well, this would help her and it would help me from mentally imploding. Please?"

When we hang up, the effects of Mom's energy-draining zapper kick in.

Bea returns from the kitchen with a piece of toast in her hand. "What's the saying? Loose lips sink ships."

I look at her sideways. "Sorry. I hope I didn't get you in trouble."

She sits next to me and nudges my arm. "You didn't. Anyhow, it'll be fun, you and me, a couple of working gals. You'll love it there. It's the best restaurant in town."

I lean my head on her bony shoulder. That's what I like about Bea. She never gets mad at me, and she always finds the sunny side in a bad situation. I've heard my mom complain to my dad that the problem with Bea is her glass is "impossibly half full" all the time. I don't understand what's wrong with that.

Bea's forehead creases as she realizes her couch is clean. "Where'd all my stuff go?"

"Oh, I thought I'd organize it for you." I show her my neat stacks and categorized piles.

"Uh-huh," she says evenly. "Hey, why don't you hop in the shower first, and then we'll figure out what you're going to wear to work."

"Okay."

Before I go upstairs, I rinse out my bowl and load it in the dishwasher. It bothers me that my mom always sticks her nose into everything, but at the same time, maybe working at the Cod Café won't be so bad. I mean, I've never had a job before. What's so wrong about a few extra dollars in my pocket?

"You know what, Bea?" I call over my shoulder. "You're right. This will be fun."

"Bea?"

She's gone. And all the junk I cleared off has returned right back to where it was.

CHAPTER 5

WORK WITH ME, PEOPLE

The Cod Café has always been a local hangout for fishermen, a place where they swap stories over morning coffee or get a hot meal after a long day at sea. But in summer, the tourists take over, and the adjoining gift shop opens to sell fish-print hoodies, fridge magnets, and rainbow geodes.

A blackboard at the entrance greets us with the lunch specials written in block letters: $12 – FRIED CLAMS SPECIAL. $14.99 – LOBSTER ROLL. Ship wheels and fish nets decorate the walls, along with framed photographs of some of the locals posing with their biggest catches. There's even one of my grandpa showing off the huge striper he caught in a fishing tournament.

Bea and I hustle into the kitchen so she can clock in. I take a moment to smooth out my light blue T-shirt and tan Chino shorts, the closest thing I have to the Cod Café uniform of navy collared shirt and khaki pants. My friend Zoe once told me that her older sister makes crazy money waiting tables, so

I made sure to wear something with roomy pockets for all the dollars I'll be stuffing in there.

A wiry, bald man with beady eyes approaches us. Bea grabs him by the arm before he passes. "Ray, this is my granddaughter, Shayne."

"Thank you for hiring me, sir," I say in my most grown-up voice.

Ray's eyes flicker between his clipboard and me. "Right . . . to be clear, I can't put you on payroll. You're not old enough—child labor laws and all. I don't want to get in any trouble. Think of this more like community service."

My ego deflates just like my empty pockets.

He snaps his fingers at a nearby waitress. "Shadow Katie," he says to me. "Do whatever she says, and don't get in anyone's way."

Katie's ponytail swings in time with her bouncy step. I quicken my pace to keep up with her as we make our way to the hostess stand at the front of the restaurant.

"Love your bracelets," she says.

"Thanks, I made them myself," I say, picking at the loose ends of the knots.

She nods with approval, and my shoulders relax for the first time today.

"Do you live around here?" I ask.

"I go to college nearby, but I grew up in Boston," Katie says as she pulls out a shoebox from the top shelf of the hostess stand. She leads me to a nearby empty booth and dumps a mess of lobster bibs, cracker packets, hand wipes, loose crayons, and a spool of twine onto the table. "If you could arrange this neatly somehow, that would be *huge*."

"No problem. I can do this in my sleep."

She winks at me. "Great. I'll be back to check on you in a few."

I settle into the booth and jump into my assignment, ready to do it right and make Katie like me. I separate everything into piles and use pieces of twine to tie sets of three crayons together in tidy packages. Each crayon bunch has different colors in it. I remember how it stunk when you were given a coloring mat but all you had to draw with was brown.

I look around for Bea. She's at one of the tables, writing furiously on a little notepad. Then she disappears into the kitchen and comes out minutes later with a large tray perched on her shoulder. Steam rises off the red boiled lobsters and baked potatoes oozing with butter. Bea tilts to one side to keep her balance, and I'm scared she's going to tip over. Katie trails close behind as a spotter. She helps Bea remove the tray from her shoulder onto a folding stand. Bea looks frazzled, her usual smile wiped off her face. She said she was excited to waitress again, but this doesn't look like excitement to me.

"I'm done," I say to Katie when she passes by. She claps her hands, which makes me feel like a preschooler.

"You are *awe-some*," she sings. "Would you want to bus tables for me?"

I shrug. "Sure, why not?"

"Perfect." She hands me a glass of water. "Give this to table four."

My blank stare gives me away.

Katie points to a corner table by the window. "See the little girl with blond braids? That one."

The glass sweats cold water, making me grip it even tighter. Great, now my hand is trembling. Why am I so nervous?

When I reach the table, I clear my throat. "Did someone order water?" My voice sounds like I need more air.

The parents cock their heads to the side to give me that *aww, isn't she cute* look. The braided toddler raises her hand. "Meeee!"

Her chubby cheeks and button eyes make me smile. "Here you go," I say, sounding at least like a human being this time. I place the glass onto the coloring mat in front of her. I so got this. But instead of saying thank you, the girl's lip quivers and fat tears spring out of her eyes.

"My picture!" she cries to her mom.

I look at her mat. Wetness from the bottom of the water glass seeps onto a few of her scribbles. I mean, honestly, calling this a picture is a stretch. But it appears I ruined the little Picasso-in-training's life, because now she is flat-out wailing.

The parents try to calm the little girl while the eyes of the entire restaurant drill into my back.

Katie rushes over with a stressed-out smile plastered on her face. "Everything okay, here?"

"Sorry," I whisper before rushing for the kitchen.

Little did I know that a kitchen during the lunch rush is like a pirate's den. It's full of fire, bubbling pots, and sweaty men wearing bandanas barking orders at each other. A cook with a sharp knife in his hand almost crashes into me. "Get the kid out of here," he yells. I back up into the dishwasher.

"Excuse me," says a tall teenage boy with stringy black hair and shiny skin.

I step aside and he opens the dishwasher. Steam engulfs my face. I can feel my curly hair expanding into a massive frizz ball.

"I can help," I say as he starts to unload. I reach in for a white plate, but it's red hot. "Ouch!"

The corners of his mouth turn up slightly. He shows me his calloused hands. "Yeah, you get used to it after a while."

"Gio!" yells one of the cooks. "Get me the sauce."

The boy's face looks intense as his arms move lightning fast to finish unloading. "I gotta get these dishes out," he replies. "They're running low in the dining room."

"I'll get the sauce for you," I offer. I know exactly what the cooks want. The Secret Sauce they put on the potato salad is legendary around here. I definitely want in on this action.

Water drips off Gio's nose. "You're a lifesaver. It's in the walk-in."

My breath quickens at the walk-in cooler's shock of cold air, but it feels amazing compared to the heat of the kitchen. I scan the shelves of gallon-sized plastic bins until I spot one with the words SECRET SAUCE written on the front with black marker. It's on a high shelf, a little above my forehead, and I stand on my tiptoes to reach it. Grabbing both sides, I slide it toward me.

It wavers. Wobbles. Whoa.

SPLASH.

It's no secret that the sauce now covers my shirt and the entire floor.

"What's going on?" Ray pops his head inside. His eyes bug out at the oily, slick mess flooding his walk-in.

I can't speak.

"Are you kidding me?" He grabs his head with both hands—to prevent it from exploding, I guess.

Gio appears like clockwork with the mop.

I start to say I'm sorry, but Ray holds up his hand traffic cop–style. "Clean it up." He exits and I can hear him yell, "She dumped the sauce," to the cooks. I feel like a complete loser.

Gio hands me the mop. I dunk it in the filthy water, and the ropey strands hang like wet hair. I make a few stabbing motions at the floor.

He laughs. "I bet you've never mopped a floor in your life."

Busted.

"Give me that." He grabs the mop and expertly works on the gooey mess.

Trust me, I've never been in love before. But at that moment, I definitely love Gio. I love him for saving my butt.

CHAPTER 6

I'D RATHER EAT ICE CREAM

"I've known Gio forever. He's in Mona's grade."

Poppy sweeps the floor in front of a refrigerated case filled with milk, eggs, pickles, and cheese. After her shift ends, we'll go to Lolli's for a double scoop of Moose Tracks ice cream. Her oldest sister, Leanne, who's eighteen and calls herself the manager, keeps a watchful eye on us.

"So . . . what do you think about him?" Poppy asks, leaning against the broom handle. A black bandana secures her thick, wavy hair away from her face.

"Who?"

"Gio. Do you like him?"

Her deep blue eyes egg me on to say yes, but instead I shrug while my gaze drifts to the dustpan.

She presses on. "He did help you out big-time, mopping up that huge mess. Do you think he likes you?"

"Doubt it."

I wish she'd drop it. When I told her about the most

embarrassing day of my life, I was hoping she'd try to make me feel better. A little *the bin was too high, could have happened to anybody*, or maybe she could tell me about something embarrassing that had happened to her, so we could both be card-carrying members of the mortified club. I didn't mean for this to be a *thing* about Gio. For the last few months, Poppy's texts have been about nothing but boys, boys, boys. It's like as soon as she finished sixth grade, someone tripped the boy-crazy switch in her brain. I was kind of hoping now that I'm up here she'd give it a rest. Hoping it would be the Summer of Poppy and Shayne. Like always.

Poppy takes off her apron and rolls it into a ball. "When I was little, I used to hate Gio because he'd call me Poopy."

I bust out laughing. "You never told me that."

"Because it's not funny."

"It kinda is . . . Poopy."

Poppy sniffs the air. "Speaking of poop, you reek of Secret Sauce. Do you have an extra shirt to change into?"

Heat creeps into my cheeks. "I wish." I sneak a sniff of my right shoulder. The smell of vinegar practically punches me in the face.

"Poppy, go see Mona," bellows her dad from behind the meat counter. Mr. Quayle is short in size but big in volume, and when he asks you to do something, you better do it. He has no qualms about yelling at his staff because they're all family. In addition to Leanne, Mona, who's fourteen, usually works the register. She's never been particularly nice or mean to me; it's more like she *tolerates* me. Like gnats in July. Or brown rice.

"What?" Poppy says to her sister, her hand on her hip.

Mona doesn't even look up from her magazine. She flicks a hand toward the produce section. "Deliveries are in."

"I'm off at three. You do it."

Mona looks at her watch. "It's 2:59. You're still on the clock."

Poppy's mouth drops open, ready to rail, but I hook her arm and drag her away. I figure the more she complains, the longer it will take for us to get out of here. So, while she groans about how she does all the work and Mona gets to read magazines and life is so unfair, I help her unload flats of strawberries and sacks of potatoes. Then we stack a crate of Gala apples into a tall, waxy pyramid.

A cowbell jangles, announcing the arrival of another customer to Quayle's Market. But it's not just any customer—it's Linc, fully dressed in his soldier costume. He blows past us and makes a beeline for the snack rack.

Pointing him out, I whisper, "That's Cranky's grandson. He and his dad showed up yesterday."

Her lip curls in disgust. "The spawn of Cranky. Barf."

"His name is Linc or something like that."

"So, you've met him," she says.

"Sort of," I say, suddenly feeling shy.

We watch him stuff his arms with bags of pretzel rods and pork rinds.

"What's with the outfit?" she asks.

I shrug. "He's always dressed like that."

Poppy rolls her eyes. "Great, another weirdo on Thomas Cove. He'll fit right in." She leans in to me and lowers her voice. "I forgot to tell you, Mona told me some more juicy bits about our Cranky. Apparently, his old house burned to the ground. She says he lost everything. That's why his new house is practically empty."

"Maybe that explains the tent," I whisper back.

"What tent?"

"You haven't seen it? Cranky makes Linc sleep outside." As soon as I say it, I feel a little guilty. I have no idea if that's really true.

"I told you he was mean," Poppy says.

"No doubt," I say. But it gets me thinking. If I lost everything in a fire, maybe I'd be cranky, too.

"Daddy, can I have one?" a sticky toddler asks as he reaches for one of our freshly stacked apples.

Poppy gasps at the same time the boy's dad says, "Don't!" but it's too late. The kid pulls a piece of fruit from the bottom tier and our whole pyramid comes crashing down.

Poppy looks like she wants to curl up under the broccoli bin and die.

"I'm so sorry," the dad says, getting on his knees. "I'll clean it up."

Poppy joins him on the floor. "Don't worry. Happens all the time." While the two of them silently collect fallen apples, I peek over my shoulder, expecting to see Linc, but he has disappeared. I poke around each short aisle and find him hiding in the bakery section. A yeasty smell fills my nostrils and my stomach responds with a growl. Linc's back is to me, so I sneak up behind him and tap him on the shoulder.

He jumps.

A blue cloth, bunched into a ball and secured with a safety pin, falls at my feet with a soft thump. I pick it up, surprised at its weight for such small thing.

"You dropped this," I say.

Fear flashes in his eyes. He grabs it from me and jams it into his pocket.

"You saw nothing," he says before he pushes past me.

"You're welcome," I call after him.

Poppy was right. What a weirdo.

CHAPTER 7

DON'T BOTHER ME, I'M ON VACATION

I'm surprised about how excited I am to go back to work. You would think I'd need more than a few days to recover from making a complete fool of myself, but I liked Katie and even Gio (even though I don't *like him* like him). Something about being in that kitchen intrigued me. It was as if we were part of *Survivor*, deranged and scary, but all in it together.

Bea said we could take *Knot for Sale* to the Cod Café today. The thought of arriving by boat makes me feel like a movie star, even though my red carpet will be a stinky wharf that smells of diesel fuel and rotted fish. I dig out a red life jacket from the heap of flashlights, tackle boxes, extra batteries, and crumpled maps. No shocker that Bea keeps the storage bin on *Knot for Sale* the same way as her house: a complete mess.

Bea pats the seat next to the outboard motor that hangs off the back of the boat. "Go ahead and start her up."

"Me?" I ask, thumb on chest.

She presses her fingers against her forehead. "Sorry, for a minute I thought you were Grandpa. My mind's going."

"No, let me do it. It can't be that hard, right?"

Bea twists her lips while she thinks about it. "You're probably too young, but what the heck. It is easy, practically dummy-proof."

"Awesome." I slide into the seat and rub my hands together. "What do I do first?"

"Everything you need is right here at the stern." Bea grips the long handle attached to the engine. "This is how we steer. You turn the end with your wrist like a motorcycle handlebar to go faster or slower. Now, to start the motor—"

"You pull the cord, right? I've seen Grandpa do it a million times."

"Good girl." Bea drapes a white scarf over her head and ties it under her chin. She puts on her sunglasses and settles into her seat as though we're going on a Sunday drive in the country.

I grab the handle and tug at the cord. I'm surprised at its resistance, so I wrap two hands around it and prop my foot against the stern's wall for balance.

"Give it a firm pull," Bea instructs.

I yank on the cord like Dad does when he starts the lawn-mower. The engine whirs with each tug, but doesn't catch. I keep pulling and pulling.

"Wait—" says Bea.

By now, it's a thousand degrees inside my life jacket, and I'm sweating buckets. I pull again and Bea grabs my arm.

"Stop!"

"What's the matter?" I ask.

"You've flooded the engine."

I sink low in my seat. "You said it was dummy-proof. More like proof that I'm a dummy."

"Relax. It happens."

"So what do we do now?" I ask.

"We wait a few minutes, then try again."

Bea folds her hands and looks at her watch. I pick at my fingernails. Across the cove, Poppy leaves her house and ducks into a car with Leanne at the wheel.

Bea's purse rings. She digs through it and removes three pairs of eyeglasses, a stack of envelopes, and a ball of yarn before finding her old flip phone.

"Hello? . . . Yes, Ray, I'm on my way." She steals a glance at me before her gaze returns to her lap. "I see . . . No, I under-stand . . . Be there in a few."

She coughs a few times and clears her throat. "Good news. You don't have to work the boring, old dining room anymore. Ray says you can help in the gift shop if you want."

"I'm fired?" First one kicked off the island.

"I thought you'd be thrilled. You didn't want to go in the first place."

"I didn't. But I didn't want to be banned either."

"Oh, honey, don't take it the wrong way. When you're a little older, and a little more mature, Ray would love to have you back."

I know she's trying to make me feel better, but the words sting. *More mature.* She pats my knee. "You'll love the gift shop. Fabulous knickknacks."

"No way. I'm not going back there, it's too embarrassing." A catch in my throat threatens to turn into waterworks. I swallow it down.

"What are you going to do then? Your mother—"

"I'll figure something out. Please . . ." This comes out as a whisper.

Bea checks her watch again. "I better go. I'm late."

I get out of the boat as Bea pulls the engine cord. It splutters to life. I help her remove the lines from the dock's posts, and she gives a gentle push off with her foot.

I wave good-bye as *Knot for Sale* putters out of the cove. Once it hits the open waters of the bay, Bea guns the engine and disappears from sight.

A hush falls over Thomas Cove again with only a squawking seagull left for company. I shuffle up the aluminum ramp at a turtle's pace, pick at the loose ends of my woven bracelets, and wonder, *What now?* Then I hear a single splash. And the loudest scream of my life.

CHAPTER 8

NO CRABS ALLOWED

I run toward the commotion and discover Linc pounding a flipped sea kayak with his fists. Even though the tide is coming in, the water's still really shallow, about knee-deep, but somehow he has managed to soak himself from head to toe. After a few moments of watching his tantrum, I kick off my Keens and enter the water. Cold grips my ankles as I churn against the current. When I reach Linc, he's shaking out one leg that's completely entangled in seaweed. His jaw is clenched so tight I'm worried smoke will spew from his ears.

"I hate the water."

"Then why are you in it?" I ask.

"Because . . ." He plucks at the rubbery strands, and, once freed, his whole body shudders. "It's my grandpa's fault. He said I had to get used to the ocean. No, his actual words were 'Get off your fat butt.' He's so mean. Can you believe he said that?"

Yeah. I can.

"He said he'd take me kayaking, so I dragged this huge two-seater kayak all the way down here. But then something broke on his lobster boat and he flipped out and had to leave to buy a new part, so here I am." He whips his head around. "Uh oh, where'd the boat go?"

"I'll get it." Water splashes up to the bottom of my shorts as I fetch the drifting yellow kayak. I turn its lightweight frame right-side up and collect the two floating paddles and extra life jacket nearby.

Linc swipes his hand through his buzzed blond hair and comes up with a sprig of seaweed. He looks at it, makes a face, and tosses it over his shoulder. "Thanks. I thought it would be easy to get in by myself, but somehow I flipped it."

"I could help you," I say.

He shrugs. "Okay."

"I'll hold the boat while you get in. I'm Shayne, by the way."

"I'm Linc, short for . . ." He unzips his life jacket to show me his wet T-shirt underneath, which features a picture of Abraham Lincoln with the words WWAD: WHAT WOULD ABE DO?

"Short for Abe?" I deadpan.

"No, Lincoln."

"Right." I smile, but he doesn't smile back. "You're lucky. I was named after an old western movie."

Linc juts out his chin. "My dad's a history teacher and Civil War expert. He's also a reenactor—he's touring with his unit right now and will be back in about a month." He kicks at the water and mumbles. "Wish I could have gone with him instead of getting stuck here."

"Are you a reenactor, too?" I ask. "You know, with the clothes and all."

"Sort of. Technically you have to be sixteen, but that's only four years away. Before we came here, my dad took me to Gettysburg for the one hundred and fiftieth anniversary celebration. You should have seen the reenactment of Devil's Den. It was amazing. You know about Devil's Den, right?"

My ankles feel numb. The best way to deal with cold water is to either keep moving or get out. "Sounds familiar, but I forget. Are you going to get in the boat or what?"

He slides into the back seat of the kayak butt-first. He's about as graceful as a sea lion on a tightrope. "How can you not know about Devil's Den? What grade are you in, anyway?"

"Seventh," I huff.

"Really?" He shakes his head and clucks his tongue. "Another example of American education going down the drain."

"Hey!"

"Just kidding," he says, putting his hands up. "I'm going into seventh, too."

Any charitable feelings I had toward this guy are quickly evaporating. I slip into the wet life jacket, which feels uncomfortably cold against my thin T-shirt. Then I ease into the front seat and position the paddle horizontally across my chest, my hands a shoulder's width apart.

"We won't tip, right?" Linc swallows hard as he clutches the side of the boat.

Not so full of yourself now, are you? "Not if you do what I say. Pick up your paddle and watch."

I dip the paddle's flat plastic blade into the water near my toes and push back firmly along the boat until I reach my hip. Then I lift the blade out of the water and do the same thing on the other side. For some reason, the kayak barely moves. I peek over my shoulder and see why. Linc's not paddling.

"*Hel-lo.* This is a two-person effort. I'm not your chauffer."

"You said to watch," he says.

"No, I meant copy me."

"Like right now?"

My jaw clenches. "I can't think of a better time."

He tilts his head and stares at the shore with a faraway look in his eyes. "You know, this place kind of reminds me of Devil's Den with all the boulders everywhere. Man, you should have seen it."

I frown. "Seen what?"

"The reenactment. It was amazing. There were sharp-shooters on the Confederate side hiding behind the rocks to try to pick off the Union solders. The fighting was fierce, but the Union defenders held their line." He shakes his head. "Over forty thousand casualties. Unbelievable."

I inhale deeply through my nose to keep me from yelling at him. "Will you paddle, please?"

Linc groans like I told him to finish his math homework. He chops the water with his paddle and splashes my side. It doesn't take long before I am as drenched as he is.

"I want to get out," he says.

"Already?"

"I don't feel well." He clutches his stomach. "Do you even know where you're going? Do you need a map? I have excellent map-reading skills."

"Why would we need a map? We've gone nowhere. And don't smack the water so much. Try a nice, even stroke."

I show him once again what to do, and this time he copies me. The kayak glides across the water as though on ice.

"That's right," I say in an encouraging teacher voice. "Nice and easy strokes. Pretend you're . . . George Washington, or something, crossing the Delaware River."

Lincoln stops paddling and winces. "That was the American Revolution."

I knew that. "Whatever. Same difference."

"No, it's not!" he yells back, red in the face.

I turn away from him so I can stick out my tongue in private. We continue to half-chop, half-paddle in silence, and I wonder what's the quickest way to end this little excursion. I don't know what I was hoping for, but hanging out with Mr. Wikipedia is absolutely exhausting.

CHAPTER 9

BE BRAVE

A couple days later, I invite Poppy over for dinner. She's been busy at the store, so we haven't gotten to hang out much. Bea and I set the kitchen table while we wait for her to arrive, which means first clearing off the stacks of newspapers, clipped coupons, and unopened mail. Bea breaks out the porcelain plates (mismatched, of course) instead of the paper we usually eat off of. She litters the table with pumpkin-scented Yankee candles but says not to light them because she doesn't want to ruin the pristine shape of the wax. If that isn't enough, chicken-bird is also making an appearance as the centerpiece tonight. It's a good thing my summer sister's coming over and not someone we want to impress.

The lid of the lobster pot clatters as the steam below threatens to escape. Poppy rings the doorbell just as the oven's buzzer sounds. Bea removes the lid with a pot holder, and a bath of steam billows to the ceiling. A briny smell fills the room as she removes the bright red lobsters with tongs.

"Wow," Poppy says as she steps into the living room. "No offense, but I've never seen this room so clean."

Bea joins us and rubs a finger across the newly revealed dark finish of the oval-shaped table. Gone is Junk Mountain; instead, along the wall are rows and rows of boxes and shopping bags with her so-called treasures—sorted, priced, and ready to be sold. While the rest of the house still has that cyclone feel to it, at least this room is packed and done. Tomorrow, all this stuff will be on display at the Cedar Island Flea Market. Yes!

I rub my tired eyes, still bleary from working on this until one in the morning the night before. For the past week, Bea had been moving at a glacial pace. She would act like she was ready to start pricing but then get distracted, or worse, blather on about how she dragged Grandpa to a yard sale and she found this *fill-in-the-blank* and it only cost *fill-in-the-blank* and she couldn't resist. Last night after she went to bed, I couldn't stand it anymore. I had to finish this myself no matter how long it took.

"Everything's alphabetized, so it'll be easy for us to stay organized," I explain to Poppy. "I marked *B* on these bags, because they're filled with books, buttons, and bear things. The *C* bag has cat stuff, calendars, and cookie sheets. *D* for dishes and dolls, you get the picture."

From one of the shopping bags, Poppy pulls out a small,

puke-yellow teddy bear. Bea pounces on it like a cat. "Oh, isn't he darling?" She plucks it from Poppy's grasp.

The thing has matted fur and smells like dirty socks. A sarcastic comment threatens to spring from my lips, but I hold it back. "I priced him at fifty cents. Is that too much? He's missing an eye, after all."

Bea cuddles the bear in her arms. "I remember when I got him. It was a Sunday afternoon. The Richters were having a yard sale, and I made Grandpa take me there after my shift. They were practically giving everything away. This little guy only cost a nickel."

Quicker than a magician, she dips her hand into another bag and lifts up a beaded necklace with a sun medallion clipped to the end.

"Pretty," Poppy says.

I throw her a look, hoping she gets my signal to keep quiet.

Next thing I know, Bea empties the entire bag on the floor and picks through its contents. She holds up the box of good luck charms. "Is it bad luck to sell good luck? Maybe we shouldn't sell these."

I seize the shoe box. "Of course we should. That's the whole point, remember?"

Bea shakes her head as if to wipe out a bad dream. "Absolutely. I need the money."

She chews on her fingernails while Poppy and I repack the bags. Then she spins on her heels and hurries to the kitchen to retrieve her favorite chicken-bird statue. "So much dust," she murmurs as she polishes its silver head with the end of her sleeve. Her eyes flicker with worry.

"Man, I'm starving," I say to change the subject.

Her gaze lingers on Grandpa's picture as she places the bird on the mantel. "Let's eat."

☆

At the kitchen table, Poppy chats nonstop, sharing Quayle's Market gossip about the pushy customers who cut the line at the meat counter, how she lost her favorite lip gloss somewhere in produce, and how all the cute boys have vanished from Cedar Island, including this year's crop of "summer people."

Bea expertly twists the lobster's tail to separate it from its body. She pushes a fork inside the narrower end of the tail, and the white meat pops out the other. She cuts off a small piece, dips it into a cup of melted butter, and hums as she chews.

"Hey, Bea, my mom said she was glad to see you back at the Cod Café. Said it wasn't the same without you." Poppy pushes her salad around her plate and leaves her lobster untouched.

Bea takes a swig from her bottled beer. "Trust me, it's still not the same. Ray's hiring all these high school kids, and they act like they're God's gift. The other day one of the dish washers—oh, what's his name—dumped a whole cup of coffee on me and didn't even say sorry. I could have killed him."

Poppy perks up. "Was it Gio?"

Bea points a fork at her. "That's right. Stupid kid."

Poppy chuckles, and I kick her under the table, even though it's the best story I've heard all day. Gio's a klutz, too. How awesome is that?

"Will you be at the flea market tomorrow?" Bea asks Poppy.

"Nah, I have to work."

"It's going to be something, all right." Bea stabs the air with her finger. "The event of the summer!"

Poppy pumps her fist and I shout, "Woo-hoo!" before we dissolve into a giggle fit. Already everything feels better. At this time tomorrow, I'll be able to walk through the family room in a straight line without tripping over something. I won't have to feel anxious anymore about where to sit, and if I want to veg out on the couch, I can do so, pile-free. I can't wait to send my mom before and after pics of the transformation. I told her I could do it. We fought Junk Mountain and won!

Bea burps and pats her mouth dry with the plastic lobster bib tied around her neck. "Girls, did I ever tell you the story about my most successful find?"

Poppy and I bite our lips to keep from laughing. Bea tells us this story every year, but Poppy pretends like she's never heard it.

"Hmm, sounds familiar, but you can tell it to me again?" she asks.

Sometimes Poppy's a better granddaughter than I am.

"Well," Bea begins, "one day I was driving along on Mountain Road when I stumbled upon a yard sale. Most of it was garbage, of course, but as I was about to leave, I spotted a vase with these lovely hand-painted wisteria blossoms against a pale green background. I knew right away it was Rosedale pottery, which is a collector's item, so I snatched it up. Probably paid five dollars for it. Meanwhile, another woman followed me to my car and offered twenty dollars on the spot to take it off my hands."

I yawn loudly, but Bea yammers on.

"Naturally, I declined. I ran home and looked up the vase on the Internet, and guess what? It was worth six hundred dollars."

Poppy slaps the table and says, "You lucky duck, Bea," which is hilarious because nobody says *lucky duck* unless you're over a hundred, and she says the same exact thing every year.

Bea beams as I clear everyone's plates.

"Maybe you'll be just as lucky tomorrow. Instead of six hundred dollars, we're gonna rake in six thousand," I say.

Her body sags a little as she takes another glance at her boxed-up things behind her. "We'll see."

CHAPTER 10

WELCOME TO THE NUT HOUSE

The next morning, we reach the elementary school to find the parking lot busy with sellers unloading their goods from their cars. Bea and I hurry our boxes and bags into the school's gymnasium. Rows of long tables divide the space, and Bea finds her name on a *Reserved* card near the entrance.

"Good spot," she says. "People will have to pass us on their way in and out."

The high ceiling carries the echoes of clinking glass, rustling paper, and metal folding chairs scraping across wood floors. We quickly arrange our table in an artful display. I wonder if her trash will look like treasure in someone else's eyes.

At the stroke of eight o'clock, the double doors fly open, and a stream of people pour inside. Hundreds of eyes scan the tables, hoping to snatch the best deals. The room feels manic, like we're selling cheap wedding dresses instead of Aunt Emily's old pot holders. It's not long before the temperature rises, and I fan my face to stay cool.

Bea sits on her folding chair like she's Queen of the Court. She waves to friends and strangers alike, hoping they will stop for a look at her fabulous offerings. I notice a few familiar faces, like Leanne, who's holding hands with her longtime boyfriend, Billy. I sink low in my chair as I spot Ray from the Cod Café browsing a few tables down. Then I see Gio and sink even lower.

"Look, Mommy," says a chubby-cheeked girl. She drags her mother by the hand to check out my friendship bracelets. Bea said I could sell them here, even though she almost choked when I told her my price of two dollars each. The girl bunny-hops with indecision as she pours over the checkered one, the zigzag one, or, my personal favorite, a black one with yellow hearts in the center. Lucky for me, the mother pipes her down by buying all three. I count the bills and stuff them in my pocket.

A man wearing a volunteer fire department shirt approaches next. He picks up a set of glass candlesticks. "How much?"

Bea clears her throat. "Fifty dollars."

My head whips around. What is she talking about? I priced those myself—five for the pair.

The fireman frowns. "Wicked expensive, lady. This is supposed to be a yard sale, not retail."

"It's crystal," Bea calls out as he lumbers away. Then she

removes the candlesticks from the table and sticks them next to her purse on the floor.

My mouth drops open. "Why did you say that? Those weren't priced fifty."

"I know, but he didn't seem like the right buyer. He probably would have chipped the glass as soon as he got home."

As the morning drags on, the excuses pile on . . . and get worse. When one woman shows an interest in a whole box of stuffed animals, Bea says, "I'd put them in the dryer first to get rid of the bugs."

A sick feeling rises in my throat. I look around the room and watch a blur of money exchanging hands. Once-full tables have winnowed down to a few remaining scraps. Not ours. Besides my bracelets, we haven't sold a single thing.

Bea excuses herself to go to the bathroom, and a few minutes later she returns with a cardboard box full of other people's junk.

I'm so annoyed I can barely get the words out. "What are you doing? We've sold nothing. The last thing we need is more stuff."

Her eyes are unfocused, like she's in a trance. "It's none of your business."

Chills run up my body at the sound of her voice, flat and robotic. I'm about to apologize, but her mood lifts as soon as she shows me her new box of goodies.

"Shayne, you're going to die when you see this." Bea hands me a rectangular piece of wood with two cartoonish squirrels painted on the front.

I read the caption aloud: *"Welcome to the nut house."*

Bea claps her hands. "Isn't it hysterical?"

"I guess, but—"

"Say no more. It's yours," she says.

I hand it back to her. "I don't need a sign, Bea, and neither do you. Your house is full of them!"

She gazes at it with moony eyes before tucking it under her chair. "You never can have too many. They're so clever!"

She can't be serious. Ever since I got here, I've been busting my butt to get her ready for this day. Now what? Was all this talk about selling her treasures a humongous lie?

I ask for a five-minute break to clear my head. As I walk the aisles, I pass a Christmas-ornament table and one full of grimy used toys. Another has a bunch of frames with family pictures still in them. I don't get it. Doesn't Bea need the money? Wasn't that the motivation for this whole project in the first place? Maybe she's overwhelmed. Money makes people go psycho. My parents stress out over it all the time. Mom works so hard to get commissions, but she always complains that there's never enough.

I stop at a table with silver dog tags, rusty canteens, and other military items. If that kid, Linc, were here, he would go gaga over this stuff.

A swatch of black velvet catches my eye. Displayed on top are five nubby things that remind me of arrowheads I've seen at a museum. I pick up one. "What is this?"

The woman behind the table looks exotic with her cat-eye makeup and jet-black hair flowing out from under a silky floral scarf.

"You're holding an actual bullet that was used in the Civil War. It is very, very old." The woman sighs. "My husband, may he rest in peace, loved to collect military paraphernalia." She glances at the ceiling and clucks her tongue. "Casper, my darling, I feel bad selling your things, but I cannot hold on to them any longer."

This definitely falls under the category of weird, I think, as I wipe my sweaty palms on my jeans, but the words *Civil War* and *old* linger in my mind. Usually ancient stuff like that has value. What if this was a hidden treasure like Bea's famous vase? Could these bullets be worth hundreds of dollars? Thousands? I bet this lady has no idea.

"How much do you want for all five?" My heart thumps against my chest.

The woman peeks at the ceiling again before answering.

"Ten dollars."

"Oh," I say with a nervous laugh. "Sorry, I only have six."

"Deal," she says.

I hand over the profits from my bracelet sale. The woman wraps the bullets in newspaper and secures the package with a piece of Scotch tape. Maybe I'm a hypocrite—buying more things after I scolded Bea for doing the same—but what if this is an ultimate find? A real, honest treasure that would solve Bea's money problems in a flash?

As I head back to our station, my excitement gives way to doubt. I picture how Bea will react to my purchase. Sure, she'll get all fired up about their possible value and may do a little research on the Internet when we get home, but then what? Will she ever resell them to make money? Probably not. She loves telling her vase story, but what she never mentions is it's still tucked away in a closet somewhere, even though she could be six hundred dollars richer. I decide not to tell her about the bullets. If they are worth something, I will find out on my own.

CHAPTER 11

MY GET UP AND GO HAS GOT UP AND WENT

In my room, I stare at the cracks in the ceiling while my mind replays over and over how we dragged everything back home. How Bea dumped all the bags and boxes back onto the table, Junk Mountain rising like a phoenix before my eyes. Afterward she bailed, rushing to work saying something about the bills not paying themselves.

Should I tell my mom? Part of me wants to. Let *her* deal with this. But that's not without consequences. She'll lash out at Bea, the two of them will fight nonstop, and I'll receive an I-told-you-so. I'd rather cause another epic spill at the Cod Café than listen to Mom tell me how she was so right, and I was so wrong.

The secret I have buried in my sock drawer finally pulls me out of bed. Holding the five Civil War bullets, I trace my finger over their pockmarks and bumpy ridges. They won't solve the mess in this house, but, gosh, what if these are worth beaucoup bucks? I've seen it happen before. On an episode of Bea's favorite TV program, *Antiques Roadshow*, a man found that the rickety old chest stored in his attic was worth over a hundred thousand dollars. Can you imagine! Even if the bullets are worth a few hundred dollars that could still help Bea big-time. I rewrap them in the newspaper and shove the little package back into its hiding place.

After a few hours, Bea calls from below. "Shayne, I'm back. I brought you some lunch."

"Be right there."

In the kitchen, Bea removes takeout cartons from a plastic bag before spilling like fifty sugar packets onto the counter. With one arm, she sweeps them into a drawer filled to the rim with an assortment of ketchup and mayo packets and other freebies she has collected from the Cod Café over the years. She then dumps a container of mac and cheese into a bowl and passes it to me. I'm about to sit down when I spot a filled garbage bag tucked under my seat.

She sees me staring. "I swung by the Donohues' house after work. They were cleaning out their garage. Look." She pulls the bag out, rummages through it, and retrieves a sleeve of panda stickers. "Do you want them?"

"No."

Unfazed, she dives back in and surfaces with a pair of high-top basketball shoes. "Barely worn," she announces.

"So? It's still gross," I say.

Bea sighs. "Well, someone's in a mood." She stuffs the items back in the bag and hauls it upstairs.

I stir the noodles in circles. What does she want me to do? Go cuckoo over every stupid thing she buys? I'm not going to pretend that this is okay.

Minutes later, Bea returns, changed out of her Cod Café uniform into a fuzzy pink robe with matching slippers.

"Shayne, I've been meaning to ask. Have you met my neighbor, Mr. Holbrook?" She joins me at the table with her own bowl of mac and cheese.

Cranky's real name makes the hair on my arms stand at attention. "No . . . why?"

"He's new to the area, but he's a lobsterman like Grandpa. Anyway, we got to talking—"

"You talked to him?"

Her brow creases. "Of course, why wouldn't I?"

She then launches into some big explanation about Maine's lobster laws, about stricter rules and regulations, and how the state has put restrictions on the number of traps a fisherman can pull in one day. Apparently, Cranky's all cranked up about it, so he's going to start offering lobster boat tours as a way to make more money.

"The problem is," Bea continues, "as he puts it—he's not a people person."

I mutter under my breath, "You don't say."

The chair scrapes across the floor as she returns her half-eaten portion to the sink. "He could really use an assistant—you know, someone to make small talk with the customers."

The word *assistant* causes a piece of macaroni to wedge in my throat.

"So I said that I had a fabulous granddaughter—"

Oh. God. No.

"—who would be the perfect helper."

My fork clanks as it hits the bowl. "Why did you do that?" She whips around, surprised at my outburst. "Because you are perfect. You're so helpful and as sweet as peach pie." I bury my head in my hands. Visions of hanging on the beach with Poppy are so far from reality, it's depressing. Let's review the activity choices to date: either wallow in my grandmother's wreck of a house, make a fool of myself in front of an entire restaurant staff, or work on a lobster boat with a raving lunatic. This is turning into the worst summer of my life.

Bea hovers over me and gives my arm a little shake. "What's the problem? If Grandpa were alive, no doubt you'd be working alongside him."

I glare at her. "He's not Grandpa. He's a stranger. Mom says never talk to strangers."

She clears my plate. "Don't be petulant. Your mother was the one who gave me the idea. She's still stuck on keeping you busy while I work, so when I told her about this opportunity, she thought it was a great solution."

My face burns. I wish everyone would stop signing me up for things without asking me first. I'm not a baby who needs to be looked after. It's insulting.

I don't care what she says, or what my mom says. I don't care if it's the greatest idea since Instagram. I'm not going.

I'm not.

CHAPTER 12

GONE SAILING

No amount of kicking and screaming did any good. I could have been first on the debate team and it wouldn't have mattered. When Bea makes up her mind, she can be as stubborn as a jammed school locker.

Fishing boats of all sizes chug in and out of the wharf at Gun Point Harbor. Captain Cranky Holbrook offers me a meaty hand, and I hope he doesn't crush mine as we shake. Splintered wood planks creak under my feet as I shift from foot to foot.

"You're going to be my deckhand, eh?" His voice is like gravel.

I nod.

"You ever been on a lobster boat before?"

I nod.

He pokes my shoulder hard. "You talk, don't-cha?"

"Yes, sir," I say, standing stiffly at attention.

"Relax," he says. "I ain't gonna bite. Can't say the same 'bout the lobsters, though." He bares his teeth.

I notice the name painted on the red hull of his boat. "Wh– why do you call her *My Way*?"

Cranky lifts his wraparound sunglasses. Etched under his right eye is a jagged scar shaped like a teardrop. "'Cause it's the only way."

Gulp.

Something behind me catches his attention, and his face morphs back into his familiar scowl. "He insists on dressing like a blasted pirate."

Linc shuffles toward us wearing his navy cap and wool button coat with a stainless-steel canteen slung around his shoulder. Even though he was the biggest pain during our kayak ride, I'm glad he's here. He might know if the bullets I bought at the flea market are worth anything.

Cranky impatiently swipes the back of his arm across his sweaty forehead. "For the last time, take off that hat."

Linc reaches for his cap. The center buckle gleams in the . sunlight. "It's called a kepi."

"I don't care what it's called. This is fishin' and we don't wear silly costumes while we fish. I need you to pay attention, no head in the clouds. You get your leg tangled up in these ropes here and . . ." He slices a hand across his neck. "Understand?"

Cranky points at me. "That goes for you, too, missy."

"Shayne," I whisper.

Linc boards the boat, removes his wool coat, and steps into an oversized pair of orange waders, which droop off his shoulders. I opt for a simple life jacket. An earlier rainstorm has turned the air thick and moist, and the thought of fog weighs heavy on my mind. I can handle any weather but that. I hate fog. Hate it, hate it, hate it.

Cranky drags a white bucket filled with silver fish on deck and checks the water-filled tank that will house the caught lobsters. The VHF radio crackles with fishermen banter, and some of the language is a bit, uh . . . salty. It's embarrassing to listen to, so I reach for the volume button to turn it down.

"Only the captain touches that," he barks.

"I didn't do anything," I say defensively.

"First rule of the sea," he announces to us. "Unless you're the captain or familiar with proper radio protocol, leave it alone. But if we start to sink, call the coast guard on channel sixteen."

Linc clutches the guardrail and swallows hard.

"Here's the drill," Cranky says over the gurgling motor. "We're going take people to Gunners Cove where we'll lift some of my traps. We catch some lobsters. We bring the folks back to shore. They're happy. They give me money. I'm happy. You two are my deckhands, my helpers. Today we'll go on a dry run, and I'll show you what's what."

Cranky pushes the throttle, which kicks the engine into high gear. *My Way* seesaws over the ocean's swells. A bolt of sunlight spears through the cloud cover, warming my body and calming my nerves. I can't say the same about Linc. His already pale face gleams vampire white.

"Are you okay?" I ask.

"I forgot to bring something."

"Bring what?"

He clutches his stomach. "Don't worry about it."

We pass a craggy coastline thick with evergreens. A black cormorant soars overhead, and I follow its flight pattern until it descends upon a rocky outcropping in the center of the bay, which is covered with hundreds of harbor seals. A few bark as we sail by, but most of them stay asleep. They look so cute with their little round heads, spotted bodies, and stubby flippers.

Cranky steers us into an inlet filled with anchored sailboats, skiffs, and dinghies. "In a few minutes, we're going to find my lobster traps, and the way we do that is to look for my buoys. Every lobsterman has his own color scheme so he can identify his traps. So look for ones with a blue top half and a gray bottom half."

Linc's eyes finally light up. "Hey, Grandpa, it's like the Union and Confederate armies living in perfect harmony."

Cranky ignores him.

"My grandfather was a lobsterman," I say to Linc.

"Oh, yeah? What were his colors?"

I start to answer, but then realize I'm not sure. Red and white? Or was it red and yellow? Yellow and orange? Ugh. I rack my brain for something, anything that would shake out the correct answer, but I can't remember and my mind's a jumble.

"My great-great-great-grandfather fought in the Civil War," Linc says, breaking the silence.

"Really?"

He nods. "Ogden Badger was his name. Second Lieutenant, Company C, of New York's 124th Infantry, called the Orange Blossom Brigade."

"Why Orange Blossom? Did they smell nice?" I snort at my own joke.

Linc doesn't laugh. "Hardly. Soldiers would go for weeks without taking a bath, and sometimes they would use the same pot for boiling food as well as their lice-infested clothes."

I cover my ears. "Gross!"

He continues. "Anyhow, Ogden Badger fought in over twenty battles, including Appomattox and Gettysburg. Remember how I told you about Devil's Den? Well, it was there where he took a bad hit. A bullet hit his arm and smashed it to pieces. Back then, of course, the way you treated a bullet wound was to amputate."

"Wait a minute. He got his arm cut off?"

"Yup," Linc says with pride. "But he survived. He was even awarded the Medal of Honor for his role in that battle." He gazes at the horizon. "I wish I'd known him." He sighs before facing me. "Why are you frowning?"

"I'm not."

I look the other way. I don't know why I was frowning. Maybe it's because he's babbling about someone he's never met and who was born over a hundred and fifty years ago. Maybe it's because he knows all these details, but I can't even come up with the colors of my grandfather's lobster buoys. And maybe it's because . . .

"My grandfather died a couple years ago," I say.

Linc studies his feet. "How'd he die?"

I swallow down the lump. "Boating accident. He drowned."

Linc's eyes moisten as he blinks rapidly. His mouth quivers. Then he barfs all over my shoes.

CHAPTER 13

SEAS THE DAY

And then there were two.

With Linc laid out like a freshly caught tuna, Cranky and I eyeball each other. I suspect he doesn't know what to make of me. He looked surprised when I didn't freak out over my vomit-covered Keens. Did I want to scream? Definitely. I died a little inside when Linc's puke touched parts of my bare foot. But something told me to stay calm, grab the hose like it was no big deal, and power wash myself knee-down.

Cranky cuts the engine. With a long rod, he lifts a blue-and-gray buoy out of the water, threads its rope through a pulley, and wraps it around a winch. He presses a button, and the winch automatically spools the rope until the lobster trap surfaces from the dark sea, strands of seaweed twisted into its wire frame. Only a tiny crab and an empty soda can are inside. Cranky removes them from the trap. He throws the crab back into the ocean and tosses the can into the garbage bin.

"I keep the traps in the water for about three nights before I haul them up," he explains. "Now we're going to remove the old bait bag and put in a new one."

Cranky unties a mesh bag hanging inside the trap and dumps stinky, decomposed fish into the sea. Hovering seagulls dive-bomb onto their newfound snack. "I'll need you to grab some herring and fill the bait bag for me."

I eye the white plastic bucket filled nearly to the rim with silvery fish, each about six inches long. They look like sardines on steroids.

"Do you have gloves or something?" I ask. The herring smells like cat food left out in the sun.

Cranky slaps me on the back. "Be tough. Your hands won't melt."

I count to three in my head, hold my breath, and stick my hand in the bucket, a pool of slippery, scaly slime. I grab a couple of fish and shove them in the bait bag. A small cry of disgust slips out of my mouth, and Cranky laughs at me. I have an urge to wipe that smirk off his face with my oily hands.

We move to the next trap, and I'm excited to see what he'll pull up. I've been on my grandpa's boat a bunch of times, but whenever he gave my parents and me a ride, it was never to catch lobsters. Afternoons with him were more like wild-life cruises, searching for osprey nests (easy to find), bald eagles (once in a while), or even whales (never seen one, but still hopeful).

In trap number two, a baby lobster hangs on tight. Even though it's cute, Cranky has to throw it back. He tells me the lobsters' bodies have to be three and a quarter inches long for us to keep them. He tosses the trap back into the water, and the coiled rope shoots over the side as if it were spring-loaded.

We motor over to the third trap. "Being a lobsterman is hard work," Cranky says over the low purr of the engine's constant gurgle. "Sometimes I catch a lot, but sometimes I don't. It ain't easy, but at least I don't have to answer to anybody."

"When's the best time to catch lobsters?" I ask.

"I start my day before the sun rises. By the time most people wake up, I may have already pulled more than a hundred traps."

I peer over the side of the boat, waiting for trap number three. Anticipation hangs in the air. That and Linc's moans from the other end of the boat.

The trap holds three grown lobsters. Jackpot! Cranky grasps one firmly in his hand to show me. It flaps its tail and snaps its claws like castanets, like it can smell fear.

"Go ahead and measure it." He hands me a metal measuring gauge.

I dangle the tool over the lobster.

"Measure it from its eye socket to the end of its back," Cranky instructs. "Come closer. I won't let it bite-cha."

I do as he tells me. It measures at three and a half inches.

"It's long enough," I say breathlessly.

"She's a keep-ah," Cranky says with his thick Maine accent. "Now, before I put her in the holding tank, I have to put rubber bands on the claws so the lobsters won't attack each other."

"Can I do it, Grandpa?"

Linc squints at us with fever-flushed cheeks, but at least he's vertical.

"That's the spirit," Cranky says. "Here, grab its back, the carapace—the part just above where the tail connects to its body. That way he can't reach you with his claws. The huge one is called the crusher claw."

"No kidding," I say.

"Yup, it's a beast of a crustacean tool. The lobster crushes its prey with the crusher claw and then uses its other one—the pincher claw—to tear food apart. That's why we have to band these suckers as soon as possible." Cranky reaches for his back pocket then frowns. "Who took my bander?"

"I didn't," Linc and I say at the same time.

"Where'd I put that dang thing?" Cranky mutters as he heads to the bow to retrieve his toolbox.

"You got him?" I ask Linc. The crusher claw is large and in charge.

"Company . . . attention!" Linc jabs the lobster in the air, making its eight spindly legs wave like crazy. "Forward, march!" He bounces the lobster toward me like it's his own Civil War puppet.

"Stop it," I hiss. "Quit messing around."

"Quiet in the ranks," he says.

I shield my face with my hands. "You'll get us in trouble!"

"Hey!" booms Cranky from the bow.

We both flinch at the sound of his voice. Linc's grandfather barrels toward us, his crank-o-meter dialed up to ten. Instinctively, Linc hides his hands behind his back as if caught with an extra cookie. Problem is, in his hand is no cookie. It's a lobster, one whose cruncher claw brushes against my hand.

And clamps down on my finger.

CHAPTER 14

PINKY PROMISE

Everything unraveled after that. Me screaming, Linc yelling something about the wounded, and Cranky telling him to shut his trap.

Thanks for the memories, people.

I wiggle my pinky finger to test it out. It's not broken, but the V-shaped scratch stings when the knuckle bends.

Wrapped in a towel after a superhot shower, I lie on my bed and spy on Linc. He's been ducking in and out of his tent for the last fifteen minutes, sometimes running into Cranky's house to gather supplies, sometimes scoping the cove with a pair of binoculars. Knowing him, he's probably pretending he's a sentry, protecting his troops from the enemy. Too bad there's nobody around to indulge him in this fantasy.

Then again, if I provide him company, maybe he'll be willing to talk about my secret bullets.

I quickly throw on some fresh clothes and stuff the package of bullets in my back pocket. As I slip on some flip-flops,

I hear a clinking sound coming from Bea's bedroom. Then a crash.

"Bea?" I tap at her closed door.

She doesn't open it. "All is well. Nothing to worry about."

"Okay." I turn to leave, but then I hear her cough, a dry rat-a-tat sound that seems to last forever.

I tap again. "Are you sure you're okay?"

"I'm fine. Why don't you go outside and find something to do."

"I am. I'm going next door." I stare at the *Loon Sanctuary* sign. "Sorry for caring," I say under my breath.

☆

"Anybody home?" I knock on the canvas flap of Linc's tent.

His head appears between the folds, eyes bugging out before he scrambles to his feet.

"Who sent you?" he asks.

I roll my eyes. "Nobody. I need to talk to you."

"Is this about your finger? You're not going to sue me, are you?"

My forehead creases. "You almost maimed me for life, you know, but for now you're off the hook. There's a private matter we need to discuss."

His face clouds with suspicion, but he lets me in anyway. The tent feels about ten degrees warmer inside. A tartan blanket covers the ground picnic-style with food, books, and crinkled maps strewn about. An army cot is pushed to one side, which makes me wonder if he does, in fact, sleep here every night.

"This is some setup," I say.

He shrugs, unimpressed. "My dad gave me the tent before he dumped me off here. One of those guilt gifts, you know?"

"Where's your mom?"

"Back home in New York. My parents are divorced, and I usually spend the summer with my dad." He lowers his eyes. "Until now."

"Do you, um . . . *have* to be out here?" I ask.

"What do you mean 'have to'?"

I can't think of a gentle way to say it, so I do what I do best: blurt. "Are you allowed in your grandfather's house?"

His eyebrows touch. "What kind of question is that? Why wouldn't I be?"

"I don't know, people have funny rules sometimes." I clear my throat. "Like take off your shoes when you come inside, or . . . don't come in at all."

"That's the weirdest thing I've ever heard," he says.

I fiddle with my bracelet, wishing I kept my mouth shut. Nothing good ever comes from rumors.

"Forget it. It's not important," I say. "I need to talk to you is all."

His face softens as he gestures to the blanket. "Have a seat."

The cramped quarters make me feel a little claustrophobic. I lean against the flaps and almost fall right through.

"Are you hungry?" He offers me a tin plate.

I pick up what looks like a thick cracker. "What is this?"

"Hardtack. Soldiers used to eat it all the time. I made a batch this morning. It's only flour and water. A lot of reenactors eat it to feel authentic."

I gnaw on a corner. It tastes like an ancient brick.

"You can dip it in water if you want to soften it." He offers me a steel thermos.

I hand the plate back to him. "No, thanks. Hey, listen, I think I found something you might be very interested in."

He takes my uneaten hardtack and rips off a monster bite. I'm surprised his teeth don't shatter.

"What's that?" he asks with his mouth full.

"Five bullets . . . from the Civil War."

He sets the plate aside and brushes the crumbs off his thighs. "Show me."

I unwrap the newspaper and place it on the ground between us.

Linc pulls out a shoebox from under the cot and riffles through the contents until he finds what he's looking for: tweezers and a magnifying glass.

"They were part of some lady's dead husband's collection," I say as he inspects each one. "She wanted to get rid of everything, so she sold them to me for only six bucks, but I think they could be worth a lot of money." I pause. "What do you think?"

Linc taps his finger on his chin. "It depends. Were they fired or were they dropped?"

"I never dropped them!"

"No, what I mean is did they drop out of the weapon?"

I shrug. "How the heck would I know?"

He examines one with three rings at its base. "This one could be the .58 caliber Union Minié Ball, but then again it could be a Sharps .52 caliber."

I lean in, eager to absorb every word.

Linc removes his cap and scratches his fuzzy, blond head. "Antiques really aren't my specialty. What you need is an expert opinion. Let me do some research, and I'll get back to you."

"Okay, but promise you won't tell anyone. If these are valuable, I don't want anyone honing in on my prize."

He crosses his heart. "Hope to die."

I start to get up, but Linc stops me. "Wait . . . What if I told you I had a secret, too? Would you keep it?"

His intense stare makes me nervous, but I sit back down and nod. From his front coat pocket, he pulls out a little package of blue cloth, the same one that fell on the floor at Quayle's Market. He unhooks the safety pin at the top, and the fabric falls away to reveal a large bronze star attached to a red, white, and blue ribbon.

"This is a real live Medal of Honor," he says. "It was given to my great-great-great-grandfather in 1884 for his service in Gettysburg. I told you about his arm, but what I left out was that after he was hit, he continued to care for his wounded soldiers."

Ornate details embellish the medal. A bronzed eagle hangs from the ribbon with its wings spread. In its talons are two cannons atop eight cannonballs.

"Only fifteen hundred of these were given out to the bravest of the brave, and my ancestor was one of them." Linc stares off into space, and from the dreamy look on his face, I wonder if he's imagining the moment, maybe even pretending *he* was the one who received the medal.

"Can I hold it?" I ask, snapping him out of his dream.

"Better not. It's a family heirloom, really rare, worth a ton." He wraps the medal back in the cloth.

"Wait, I don't get it . . . What's the secret part?" I ask.

A sheepish look crosses his face. "Well, it's not *exactly* mine. I sort of . . ."—he clears his throat—"took it from my grandfather."

"You what?"

He lowers his voice. "It's complicated. There was a fire in his old house up in Belfast, and only a few things survived, including this medal. A miracle, right?"

"I guess so."

"Grandpa says he's going to give it to a museum because technically it's not his—it belonged to my grandmother's side of the family—but that's stupid. If he doesn't want it, he should give it to me."

"So, let me get this straight—instead of asking for it, you thought stealing was a better option?"

"It's not stealing; it's a temporary borrow," he snaps. "I take it out in the morning, and before I go to sleep I put it back in the desk drawer where he keeps it. You don't know him. He's not the easiest person to talk to." He grabs my arm. "Promise me you won't say anything. If Grandpa knew I was walking around with it, he'd kill me."

I wonder if he's serious. Like Cranky would really kill him. Poor Linc. No wonder he lives in a dream world of Civil War battles. It's probably the only way he can cope with the battles that must be going on in that house every day.

"Swear on it," he says. He offers me his pinky, and I interlock my scratched up one with his.

Promise.

· CHAPTER 15 ·

IS THIS DRAMA REALLY NECESSARY?

A few days later, Poppy invites me to hang out on the pebbly beach that frames the north end of the cove. Low tide peaked several hours ago, but even though the tide is coming back in, there's still a swatch of exposed sea floor left to explore. It's like this big muddy treasure chest chock-full of shiny black mussels, scurrying hermit crabs, and shimmery sea glass. Poppy and I love to collect sea glass, which is broken glass that the sea has tumbled smooth and soft. Any piece we find that's thumb-sized or bigger gets added to our stockpile. Our plan is to make jewelry out of it one day and sell it online. We're going to call our company Shoppy, a combination of our names—it's a lot better than Payne.

My eyes scan the ground. If you're not paying attention, it's easy to miss the glass among the sand, pebbles, and broken shells. So far, all I've found is a cobalt shard tangled in a nest of seaweed. Technically it's not big enough for Shoppy, but I can't resist its deep, dark color, so I pocket it anyway.

Poppy hasn't found anything either, but maybe she'd have more success if she'd concentrate. Ever since a bunch of teenage boys started splashing around in front of her neighbor's house, she's done nothing but stare at them or fuss with her bikini straps or redo the messy bun on top of her head. It's really annoying. We're supposed to be collecting sea glass. That was the plan. All the fun drains out of a plan when you're the only person who cares.

We retreat to our towels and dive into the banana-nut bread her mom baked for us. Poppy leans back on her elbows and lifts a knee into a perfect beach pose.

"Are you wearing makeup?" I ask when she removes her sunglasses. A light pink shimmer dusts her lids.

"Well, you never know when someone's going to take a picture and post it. You have to be ready."

I'm definitely not ready in my oversized Camp Red Rock T-shirt with the stretched-out collar. Who dresses up to go to the beach?

We eat our muffins in silence, and for the first time, the quiet feels uncomfortable. Every time I think of something to say, my inner censor strikes it down. A moment of panic seizes my body when I realize Poppy doesn't know about my so-called new job. I'm definitely not ready to tell her. Not only would she freak if she knew I spent an afternoon with Cranky, but if she hears that Linc threw up on my shoes and attacked me with a lobster, I'll never hear the end of it. I don't even want to tell her about the ancient bullets I found. If I did, I'd have to admit everything about Bea—how she can't part with her stuff, how she needs money, how living with her has started to feel like drowning.

"I almost forgot. I made you something." I loosen the drawstrings on my bag and dig out a finished friendship bracelet. It's a simple Chevron pattern, but I love the way the black threads pop against the pastel blue and pink. I expect her to stick out her wrist so I can tie it on, but instead she grips mine.

"OMG. Your boyfriend's here."

She flicks her head toward the group of boys. Gio stands on a boulder a couple feet above the water's edge. Wearing his Cod Café uniform, he's the only one not in a bathing suit. The other boys kick water at him and goad him to jump in. Gio mimics a diving stance and pretends to launch. Someone from the pack clucks like a chicken. He backpedals a few steps; maybe he changed his mind. Then without warning, he flings himself into the water fully clothed. The boys whistle and cheer.

When he surfaces, Poppy waves her arms over her head. "Gio, over here."

My stomach twists into a pretzel. I cover her mouth with my hand, which she pushes away.

She spits. "Gross, you got sand in my mouth."

"Cut it out, *Poopy*."

As soon as the words slip out, her eyes narrow into slits, and I instantly regret it. She's mad at me.

I lower the lid of my baseball hat to hide my heated face. Why does she want to embarrass me? I never, ever, said I liked him. Not once. I happen to mention his name one time and she acts like I want to marry the guy.

"Land! Land!" we hear someone scream from the far end of the beach. Linc runs through the water, splashing everyone nearby while Cranky tugs the yellow kayak onto shore. Linc crawls onto the sand and kisses the ground. Then, like a mosquito to an ankle, he spots me instantly.

"Shayne!"

Ugh. Why now? His little costumes never really bothered me before, but suddenly he looks like such a freak with his hat and canteen. How does he not get beaten up every day at school?

Linc stands in front of us in a wide stance like he's trying to steady his sea legs. Poppy's eyebrows scrunch while I busy myself with the important task of separating grains of sand.

He points to the horizon. "Did you see us? We paddled all the way to the end of the cove. For some reason, I wasn't scared this time. Wonder why?" He pats his front pocket and winks at me.

The stupidity of it all hurts my brain. Not only are his winks painfully obvious, but he thinks that kayaking with Cranky's precious medal is a good idea. What if he capsizes and dumps it into the water? For someone who thinks he's so smart, he is completely dumb.

"I'm Linc, by the way." He salutes Poppy, which makes me wish quicksand would silently suck him away from here.

She puckers her lips into a sour face. "Can you move? You're blocking my sun."

He scooches out of the way and flops down next to me.

"I meant farther than that," Poppy mutters.

Linc ignores her and talks out the side of his mouth. "I have information." Again with the winks.

I clear my throat. "Not now."

"What?" Poppy asks, even though she can barely tear her gaze away from the boys on the dock.

Linc starts to say something, but I elbow him in the ribs and mouth the words *shut up*.

"But what about that thing?" he says.

Poppy turns to us with an eyebrow raised to the sky. "What thing?"

I shrug my shoulders. "I have no idea what he's talking about."

"Yes, you do," he says.

Poppy wraps a protective arm around me. "We're kind of busy right now," she says to Linc. "Maybe you should go back to your side of the cove and play dress-up by yourself, or whatever it is that you do."

Her insult stabs him like a bayonet at Gettysburg. Linc jerks to his feet, sending sand everywhere. "Never mind," he mumbles before looking me square in the eye. "I suffer from amnesia. I forgot *everything* I was going to say."

His shoulders hang as he lumbers back to the other side of the cove. Poppy shakes her head and exhales a big *what-ever* before her focus drifts back to Gio and the gang.

Part of me wants to say something to her to get back in sync, but the quiet stays wedged between us while I think about my hidden treasure sitting in my drawer, gathering dust.

I totally blew it.

CHAPTER 16

SALTWATER CURES ALL WOUNDS

For our first official lobster boat tour, I stand beside Cranky as we welcome aboard ten customers—three couples and a family of four. I was hoping Linc would be here, as well, so I could apologize for acting like a jerk the other day, but Cranky told him to stay home. He didn't want to risk him barfing all over people's shoes.

It's a perfect day for cruising Casco Bay, with sunny skies and calm wind. As he did on our run-through, Cranky drives us to Gunners Cove and gets to work hauling one of his traps. All eyes watch the water for the trap to surface. Inside are two baby lobsters plus one that looks to be a keeper. Cranky tosses the little ones overboard and examines the biggie. When he turns it over, we see a tail covered in what looks like thousands of tiny black pearls. He explains to the group that they're eggs; we've caught a female lobster, and she has to go back. It's the law.

Hovering seagulls screech as they compete for the old bait bag remains dumped into the sea. As I reach for some fresh herring refill, Cranky says, "That's okay, Lobster Bait, you've passed initiation." He tosses me a pair of black rubber gloves.

Lobster Bait, huh. Not the seafaring nickname I was hoping for, but if that's what it takes to get gloves around here, fine by me.

The next two traps come up empty, but the third has three big lobsters inside. The customers clap as Cranky pulls a gigantic one out of the trap. Water drips off its gleaming brown shell.

"Ready to get back on that horse?" He offers me the banding tool, which looks like a pair of pliers with a thick yellow rubber band wrapped around the top.

I shake my head furiously. "You do it."

He grabs my wrist so quickly that a frightened squeak slips out my mouth. A woman with binoculars around her neck leans in, frowning, but I smile at her to let her know I'm fine. Cranky's eyes may be hidden behind his dark wraparound sunglasses, but I can feel them boring into my skull.

"Now listen up," he says to me low and quick. "You may think, 'Oh, a lobster hurt me. I can't handle it. Boo-hoo.'"

"I didn't say that," I hiss.

He holds up his hand to shush me. "*Or*, you can show 'em who's boss. If there's one thing you should know about it me, it's this: I'm not big on quitters."

The lobster stares at me with its beady little eyes and snaps its claws as if to prove a point. Sure, I remember how bad it hurt to get pinched, but I also remember this lobster's friend, the one I ate at dinner the other night.

"Give me that," I say as I take the bander from Cranky. One squeeze makes the rubber band stretch open. I slip it over the lobster claw, twist the tool, and release. The claw is closed, banded, and done. I must have looked relieved, because everyone applauds.

Take that, you crazy crustacean!

As we head back to the wharf, Cranky cuts the engine so the group can take pictures of Pemaquid Point Lighthouse. Maine has a ton of historic lighthouses up and down its coast, but this particular one is classic, perched on a high cliff with its dark lantern and stark white tower. This lighthouse is so famous that its image is featured on the back of the state quarter.

Cranky and I lean against the lobster tank he keeps on deck, already halfway full with today's catches.

"Have you been a lobsterman your whole life?" I ask.

He scratches the gray stubble on his chin. "Pretty much. I tried landscaping for a little while, and one summer I drove a cement truck. But my father was a fisherman, and his father before that. So eventually, I settled into the family trade." He cocks an ear to listen to the marine radio, full of chatter. "Coast guard's busy today."

"Why? What's happening?" Sea breezes fill my nostrils with a fresh, clean smell.

"Sounds like someone ran his boat aground into a sandbar."

I snort. "What an amateur."

He doesn't laugh along with me. "Boating's not easy out here, that's for sure. You've got to navigate around hundreds of buoys, you have to remember to check the tides, and then there's the weather. Fog can appear and disappear quicker than a magic act."

Hearing the word *fog* makes my insides churn.

"If you don't know what you're doing, it's easy to get into trouble," he says.

"My grandpa had an accident in the fog," I say softly. "A fatal one."

Cranky looks at me sideways.

"Another boat collided with his, and it knocked him over the stern. He fell into the water and hit his head on a rock. It was a freak accident. Could have happened to anybody. At least, that's what everyone tells me."

"I know about accidents, believe me." He grips the handrail and gazes out to the horizon.

"The fire?" I ask in a small voice.

Cranky turns to me and frowns. "Is that your business?"

"No, sir," I say, staring at my feet.

My Way rocks over the gentle swells. I widen my stance to keep my balance.

"Fire marshal ruled it accidental," he says after a moment. "Faulty wiring on a porch light. I was out at the time it started, and when I came home, the whole place was up in flames. When I ran in to see what I could salvage—"

With wide eyes, I interrupt. "You ran into a burning house?"

He shrugs. "Maybe not my smartest move, but there was this thing I had to try to save. Something that belonged to my late wife that she cherished."

The Medal of Honor! Linc said only a few things survived the fire, so that has to be what he's talking about. I can't believe he risked his life for it, and I can't believe Linc thinks it's okay to take it without asking. I don't care if he's mad at me; when I see him again, I'm really going to let him have it.

"I'm sorry about your house, Cranky," I say without thinking.

He freezes before slowly turning to meet my gaze. "What did you call me?" His eyebrows practically touch.

The blood drains out of my shocked face. Please tell me I did not call him Cranky to his face. For a crazy second, I think he's going to hurl me overboard, but instead he starts to laugh, slow and low, which gains in speed until he's slapping his leg and hacking a smoker's cough.

"My wife used to call me that, because she said I was the

crankiest SOB she'd ever met. Still loved me, though, for forty-two years."

He removes his sunglasses and presses a fist to the corner of his eye. I can't tell if the tears are from laughing or crying, but it doesn't matter. I'm still horrified.

He's about to put his sunglasses back on but winks at me first. "Let's get this boat to shore so I can get paid."

After a series of group pictures, Cranky and I run down our cleanup checklist before heading home. We bounce along the winding roads in his rattling pickup truck, silent but comfortable, like two tired fishing buddies after a fruitful day at sea. As we pull into his driveway, I see Linc waiting at the bottom of the porch steps dressed from head to toe in reenactor regalia: long navy coat with gleaming gold buttons, sky blue trousers, and, of course, his trusted kepi. I glance at Cranky, wondering if this will thoroughly irritate him, but his bored expression doesn't change.

As we exit the truck, Linc walks toward us with a huge smile on his face. He looks different, taller. My eyes flicker to something on his jacket. Pinned on front is his great-great-great-grandfather's Medal of Honor for everyone to see.

CHAPTER 17

KEEP YOUR EYE ON THE BALL

On the rickety steps of Cranky's porch, Linc fills me in. Turns out, this morning Cranky gave him the medal to wear for the day as a sort of consolation prize. He felt bad about telling Linc to stay home. (Not that Linc felt badly at all—being banned from *My Way* was like winning the Battle of Vicksburg. His words, of course.)

"Isn't it awesome," he says, sticking out his chest. The weight of the medal tugs at the wool coat.

"I'm glad you don't have to sneak around anymore," I say. "Your grandpa told me everything about the fire."

Linc looks shocked. "He did?"

"Mmm-hmm," I say smugly. "The relationship between captain and deckhand is one of mutual trust."

He sticks a finger in his mouth and pretends to throw up.

At that moment, Bea steps out of her house with several shopping bags draped off each arm. "You're back," she calls out as she approaches us.

"That your grandma?" Linc whispers.

"Yep."

He points to the bags. "What's she got in there?"

I sigh. "Who knows?"

"You must be Linc. I'm Bea, nice to meet you."

He jumps to his feet. "Do you need help? That's a lot of stuff you're carrying."

"Well, aren't you a gentleman." Bea's eyes twinkle with excitement as she sets the bags on the ground. "The Baslers were having a yard sale, and it would have been rude if I didn't see what they had to offer." She digs into one of the bags and pulls out a Nerf football with a chewed-off tip. Must have been a dog toy.

She hands it to Linc. "Here."

"Um . . . thanks?" He gapes at it like it's an alien baby.

"You're welcome." She grasps the handles once again and clomps up Cranky's porch stairs.

"What are you doing?" I ask.

"Being neighborly. I found a New England Patriots baseball cap. Never worn. Maybe he'd like it as a housewarming gift."

"Why do you think he would want a hat?"

"Why wouldn't he? It's free!"

I bury my head in my hands as Bea lets herself inside with a "Yoo-hoo, hello!"

Linc looks at the football. "Interesting."

"Very."

He laughs and for the first time I notice the dimple in his chin.

"What am I supposed to do with this?" he asks.

I snatch it from him. "Duh, throw it."

As I suspected, Linc can't catch a ball to save his life. You would think the football was a greased watermelon; he either bobbles or drops it. One time, the ball smacks him right in the chest and he falls over in slow motion. I'm beginning to wonder if he's clowning around on purpose.

"So, listen," Linc says after he picks himself off the ground. "I forgive you for your rudeness the other day." He holds up a hand to shush me before I can protest. "What I wanted to tell you was I found this place on the Internet called the Soldier & Saber. It specializes in military antiques, and you can bring in stuff to get it appraised—you know, to see how much it's worth."

My pulse quickens. "Really?"

"Even better," he says, "Grandpa said he'd take me there after dinner, so I can stock up on reenactment gear. So, either I can ask about the bullets for you, or you can come with us." He stops himself, as his ears turn pink. "That is, if you want to."

"Are you kidding? I definitely want to go. Thank you so much!" Before I know what I'm doing, I throw my arms around him in an epic bear hug. He doesn't return the hug and when I step back, he looks totally spooked.

Behind me, a throat clears.

Poppy's blue eyes are wide with disbelief. My face heats to a thousand degrees and Linc's looks like he landed on the sun.

"We were throwing a football around," I explain idiotically.

"In what century?" She makes no effort to hide her disgust with Linc's outfit.

"Do you want to play?" I ask, wanting to change the subject.

She pauses, then shrugs. "Sure, why not?"

We stand in a triangle formation and throw the ball to each other, but unlike a few minutes ago, no one is having any fun. In fact, I can tell Linc is trying his hardest not to make a mistake. I only wish he wouldn't make that *oof* sound every time he makes a catch.

Once, when Linc throws it to me, Poppy says to him, "No offense, but you throw funny."

The stricken look on his face makes me mad. "Poppy, don't be mean."

She jams her hands on her hips. "I'm not being mean, it's a fact. He's not using his legs. Shayne, give me the ball."

I toss it to her.

"You need to step into the throw," she instructs while winding her arm back behind her ear. She takes a step and launches a perfect spiral to Linc. I see him raise his hands, but the next thing I know, he's writhing on the ground in pain.

I rush over to him. "What happened?"

"Jammed my finger," he says in a strained voice.

"Maybe you need ice," Poppy says.

Linc glowers at her. "Yeah, maybe."

☆

Poppy waits until Linc is safely inside before she goads me. "I didn't know you and the tent troll were, like, besties."

"I've gotta go." I turn to Bea's place, but Poppy grabs hold of my arm.

"I'm kidding. Can't you take a joke?"

I whip around and throw my hands in the air. "Just because you don't like Cranky doesn't mean you should take it out on Linc. He's a Civil War reenactor, and he takes it very seriously. That doesn't make him a bad person, you know."

Poppy's face softens. "Look, let's not get into a fight over some boy. We've got more important things to discuss."

I narrow my eyes. "Like?"

"Like the Cumberland Fair. It's in town, and Leanne said she'd take us tonight."

Drat! Why tonight? I love the Cumberland Fair. Rickety rides, tractor pulls, cheesy games. Poppy and I go every summer. How can I miss it? But I already told Linc I'd go with him to the Soldier & Saber. Then again, he could go alone. He already said he'd ask about the bullets for me. But if they're worth a ton of money, shouldn't I be there to hear it first?

"I don't know," I say, still debating the thought in my head. "There's this thing I was supposed to do."

"What thing could be more important than the fair? Word has it there's a new ride this year called the Vomit Comet."

"Lovely."

"Come on, how can you not want to go? It's tradition, just you and me."

Tradition. You and me. We certainly haven't had a ton of that. If I say no, I might not get another chance.

"If you make me go alone, I'll die." Poppy bows her head. Her hair falls across her face like a closing curtain before she crumples to the ground with her tongue stuck out in an elaborate, twitching death scene.

She's so over the top that I have to laugh. "Fine, you win. I'll go."

Poppy springs up like a jack-in-the-box. "Cool, see you later, then."

"Okay, see you later."

She turns and tosses the football over her shoulder, and I wonder if I made the right choice.

CHAPTER 18

STEP RIGHT UP TO THE FREAK SHOW

"Let's meet back here at ten o'clock," Leanne says. She adjusts her straw cowboy hat over her bleached blond hair.

We're standing at the ticket kiosk at the fair's entrance.

"Where are you going to be?" I ask.

"Away from you guys." She laughs as Billy threads an arm around her waist and ushers her toward the main grandstand to watch the tractor-pull contest.

A fireball sun hangs at the edge of the horizon. Poppy stuffs a wad of Admit One tickets for the rides into her pink wristlet. Her bare shoulders glisten with sweat even though she's wearing a tank dress. The air is still and sticky and smells like a cross between fried dough and a barn. When you're away from the water, you miss that breeze.

We study a map of the fair and decide to head toward the midway. Tattooed barkers call to us, promising an easy win if we play milk-bottle toss or dart balloons. Oversized stuffed animals dangle from the ceiling, and suddenly I *have* to have a giant purple monkey. I blow through a bunch of dollar bills until I finally win a prize at the whack-a-mole game: a stuffed banana wearing sunglasses and dreadlocks.

After downing a corn dog and sugary lemonade, I am amped up for a ride on the giant slide. We climb the tall staircase with burlap sacks slung over our shoulders and let a few people go ahead of us until two lanes open where we can sit side by side and race. I keep my hands up the whole time even though the first drop threatens to bring the corn dog back up. Afterward, we hit the Sea Serpent, one of our favorites. It's a giant swing in the shape of a pirate ship that rocks back and forth. We sit in the back row where the motion feels the most intense and scream our heads off. Then it's off to the bumper cars where I make it my personal mission to smash Poppy.

By now, the sun is down and the neon lights are up. Families with small children head to the exits while teenagers show up in packs. We walk arm in arm by the deep-fried Twinkies stand when Poppy stops in her tracks.

She grips my elbow. "Gio's here."

I twist my neck to see a group of five boys by the fortune-teller tent. They stand in a semicircle, hands stuffed in their pockets and baseball hats turned backward or sideways. Gio, wearing a black T-shirt and camo shorts, is the tallest of the bunch.

"Go talk to him," Poppy urges.

"No way," I say.

"Come on, what are you afraid of?"

"I'm not afraid. If you want to say hi so bad, do it yourself."

Poppy flips her hair off her shoulders and looks deep into my eyes like I'm her personal mirror. "How do I look?"

"Possessed."

She sticks out her tongue at me before sauntering over to the group. My head starts to hurt. What is she going to say to him? I retrieve berry lip gloss from my purse to busy myself. Out of the corner of my eye, I see Poppy returning with Gio right behind her.

Great.

Gio acknowledges me with a *'sup* before he and Poppy decide they want to go to the trailer turned haunted house. I quicken my steps to keep up with them.

A shaky wooden bridge leads us into a dark room. Robotic monsters jump out of the shadows. Ghoulish moans pipe through speakers.

"It's not that scary," I say into the darkness. No one responds.

We pass by fun house mirrors. Gio has compressed to two feet tall. He flaps his stubby T. rex arms, and Poppy laughs like it's the most hilarious thing on the planet. It's not *that* funny. We continue through a dark corridor into a room full of stringy cobwebs where a furry puppet spider drops from the ceiling inches away from our faces. Poppy screams and leans into Gio for safety.

"It's so fake," I say, but they're still not listening to me. Poppy is too busy doing whatever she can to touch Gio. She's slapping his shoulder. She's covering his eyes. She's acting like a pesky fly. If I were him, I'd swat her.

After the lame, not-haunted house, Poppy fidgets with indecision over what to do next. I suggest the Ferris wheel, which looms over the fair like a giant centerpiece.

"Ladies first," the ride operator says to Poppy and me when it's our turn to get on. Poppy gets in, then me, then Gio. I'm sitting between them. And I really feel weird.

"Wait," I say. "I have to get off."

Poppy tugs at the hem of my miniskirt. "Why, what's wrong?"

"I'm afraid of heights. What was I thinking? You guys go ahead and I'll wait for you at the exit."

"Are you sure?" Poppy asks as I step out of the car.

Gio scooches next to Poppy so close she's practically in his lap.

I'm sure.

I walk to the nearest food stand to buy a bottle of water. A group of girls who look to be my age pass by. I think about my friends back home. If they were here, we would ride that Ferris wheel together, and no one would mind the middle seat. It's the Ferris wheel, not the third wheel.

I look at my dreadlocked banana. "Guess it's you and me tonight," I say. I try not to look alone and pathetic, but then again, I'm talking to a banana.

After a few *loooong* minutes, Poppy and Gio's orange car descends slowly to the bottom. The operator reaches for the latch to the door, but Gio says something to him and he pauses. Gio points at Poppy, who has a goofy grin on her face. I can't hear how the man replies, but he steps away from the car and lets them go for another ride.

"Oh, come *on*." I pull the map out of my purse to see what else I can do to kill time. A nearby barn seems like a quick way to keep busy. Goats and sheep greet my entrance with a chorus of *mehs* and *baahs*. Bored cows swish their tails. The hay-covered floor feels soft under my high-tops.

I give a farmer lady a quarter for some animal feed. The goats shove each other to get to my open, flat palm full of brown pellets. A black one with a white tuft between its ears wins. Its tongue tickles my hand as it laps up the food.

After a squirt of hand sanitizer, I enter a pen where you can hold and pet baby bunnies. I almost have a heart attack when I see Linc sitting on a hay bale with a white bunny in his lap.

I tap his shoulder. "Did you go to the Soldier & Saber?"

He shakes his head. "Grandpa said we should take advantage of the fair while it's still in town and go to that store another time."

When he finally looks up at me, his eyes are as red as the bunny's. I sit next to him. "Are you okay?"

"I can't find it. I've looked everywhere," he whispers.

"For what?"

Linc shuts his eyes and winces. "The medal."

My hand covers my mouth.

"I was going to return it before we came here. Then I looked and . . . it was gone, just two holes left in my jacket from the pin." His voice wobbles.

I run a quick mental inventory of the afternoon. He definitely had it on while we hung out at Cranky's place.

"Does your grandpa know?"

"Not yet. I'm dead."

He steals a glance over at Cranky, who leans against one of the stalls, the New England Patriots hat, the one Bea gave him, pulled low over his eyes. I'm not sure, but he may be sleeping.

"Don't panic. What we need to do is retrace your steps. What were you doing before you came here?"

He releases the bunny from his lap. "I had dinner."

"And before that?"

"I was in the kitchen icing my finger. Before that, you and I were throwing the football with that friend of yours."

I summon my mind for a clear picture of us outside. Did he have the medal on his jacket then? I don't remember anything unusual, except for his horrible catches.

My eyes widen. His horrible catches.

"Remember how you kept falling down?"

Linc nods slowly while he thinks about this. "Maybe the pin got knocked loose." He jiggles his legs ups and down with nervous energy. "You think it's in the grass? I want to go home and check right now."

"It's too dark. I'll help you look first thing in the morning." I slide an arm around his back and give him a half hug. "Don't worry, we'll find it."

His shoulder presses into mine. "Thanks."

An uneasy, nagging feeling tugs at my insides, like I'm forgetting something.

Blood rushes to my ears. "Ohmigod, how long have I been here?"

Linc shrugs. "I don't know."

"I have to go." I dash out of the barn and thread my way through a thick crowd to the Ferris wheel's exit gate. No Poppy. I back up a few steps and crane my neck as I check each car. No one looks familiar. This is not good.

I dig for my phone. The black screen makes me curse myself for forgetting to check the charge. How stupid am I? *Breathe, Shayne.* Where would they have gone? On another ride, back to the midway, to the tractor pull? I can't think straight.

I jog to the barn. The bunny pen has cleared out, and Linc and Cranky are gone. I head to the Ferris wheel again. With each step, my heart beats louder, almost overtaking the hum of the crowd. *Where are you?* I walk the entire length of the fair until a chain-link fence welcomes me to a dead end. I spin on my heels and dive back into the crowd. I can't believe it. She *left* me!

CHAPTER 19

KEEP CALM AND CALL YOUR MOM

Every minute that passes inches me closer and closer to full-on freak-out mode. Midway barkers yell, trying to get me to play their ridiculous rip-off games. I lean the stuffed banana against a metal trash barrel with the hope some lucky kid will claim it. Now, I'm looking for a cop, security guard, or even a kind mom with a cell phone to help me. I pass the haunted house, turn a corner, and practically collide head-on into Poppy.

"I texted you a million times," she fumes.

"My phone died." I'm about to hold out my arms for a hug, but she lays into me instead.

"Where'd you go? You said you'd wait for us. Gio took off, by the way. He didn't want to stick around and do a whole search party thing."

I can't believe she's mad. "I was only gone a few minutes. You weren't there when I came back."

Poppy exhales an irritated breath. "Then you should have gone to the ticket booth like Leanne said."

"I thought you left."

Her glare is ice. "Like I'd really leave you here. Is that what you think of me?"

"No." My voice cracks, and I can't hold it any longer. A big sob shakes my body.

She turns her back on me and marches toward the exit. Through my tears, I watch the heels of her sandals kick up little puffs of dust.

☆

When they drop me off, only Leanne says goodnight. The car pulls away, leaving me alone at the doorstep of Bea's darkened house. Moths keep me company as they flutter in circles around the dim porch light. While I fumble for the key, a beam of light sweeps across Cranky's yard.

I hug myself against the night's chill. "Linc, is that you?"

The light pauses, then flips up into my eyes. "Can you help me?" he shouts. "I can't wait till morning."

Linc trains the beam of the flashlight along the ground while I join him on his search. We zigzag across the lawn without talking, moving back and forth in strips like a human lawnmower. It's not long before my mind wanders, Poppy's words replaying over and over in my head. *Is that what you think of me?*

Well, I don't know what to think anymore. You didn't seem to care that I was lost, that I almost passed out from panic. You couldn't get over that I ruined your time with Gio.

Linc drops to his knees and fans his hands over a swatch of grass. "I was standing here most of the time, wasn't I?"

I kneel beside him and run my fingers through the blades, even though my head is still elsewhere.

I guess Gio's more important than me. You never used to yell at me. Now, whatever I do seems to bother you. What changed?

Who am I kidding? Everything has changed.

"Argh, where is it?" says Linc, now crawling with the flashlight wedged in his mouth.

"Don't worry, we'll find it. We'll look again in the morning if we have to. Wait, scratch that, another tour group is scheduled for nine-thirty. Also, when were you thinking about going to the Soldier & Saber?"

"I don't know," he says between clenched teeth.

"Tomorrow afternoon I am totally free. I can definitely come with you this time."

He spits the flashlight out. "If you haven't noticed, I can't deal with that right now. I have some problems of my own."

☆

I do my best not to wake Bea as I climb the stairs. Out my bedroom window, the beam from Linc's flashlight continues to bounce around the yard. Forget him. I've had enough bad attitudes for one night.

Wide awake and fidgeting under my covers, I wonder if I should call my mom. I know it's late, but maybe she's still up. Even though things aren't the best between us, I really want to talk.

After two rings, she answers.

"Did I wake you?" I ask.

"I wish you had, but no," Mom says. "I just got home."

"Where were you?"

"Believe it or not, at my client's house. She's an older lady, and I sat in her kitchen for hours as she wrung her hands about an offer on her house. It's ten thousand over the asking price—"

"That's good, right?"

"It's amazing. But the finality of it was freaking her out. She's lived in that house for thirty years and was having a hard time letting go. Eventually I convinced her to accept the offer, hallelujah. Now I have to get the contract ready."

A kettle whistles in the background. No doubt she's preparing her nightly cup of peppermint tea before going to bed. Suddenly, I really miss home.

"That's great news, Mom."

"Thanks," she says, pausing to sip her drink. "I've been meaning to ask you, how'd the flea market go?"

A sense of dread overtakes me as I realize we haven't spoken since. I don't want to lie to my mom, but I already blew

Bea's secret about going back to work. I can't tell on her again. She'll never forgive me.

"Uh . . . it went well! I sold some of my bracelets, so that was awesome." A series of my nervous yawns interrupt our conversation—a thankful break from revealing the truth. "Anyway, today I went out on Mr. Holbrook's boat again, and he says I'm doing a great job. I wish you could see me, Mom. You would be really impressed."

"I wish I could see you, too. I remember when I used to be Grandpa's deckhand."

This catches me by surprise. Mom never talks about when she was a kid. I assumed she was born an adult.

She continues. "I think I was nine or ten. Grandpa said it was time for me to pull my weight around the house, so he made me get up at the crack of dawn and pull traps with him. I remember complaining a lot. Grandpa wasn't used to so much talking on his boat, let alone griping. So he rewarded me by making me fill a bait bag with my bare hands."

My eyes widen. "I had to do that, too."

We laugh together. I want to know more. Did she ever get her finger pinched? Was she afraid of fog like me?

I burrow deeper under the covers. "How long did you work on Grandpa's boat?"

She sighs. "Well, back then you didn't see too many female

deckhands. I wanted to learn more, I really did, but Bea thought it best that I stay home with her."

"Is that why you and Bea . . ." I stop, searching for the right words. "You never seem to get along."

Mom pauses so long that I ask if she's still there.

"We're different people," she finally says. "When I was younger, we were close, but as I grew older, we seemed to have less and less in common. Then it was like one day I woke up and I barely knew her anymore."

Her words bring me back to Poppy and our fight. I almost forgot she's the reason I called Mom in the first place. The weight of the evening catches up with me, and the desire to sleep makes me get off the phone fast. Poppy and I aren't like my mom and Bea. We may be different people, but she's still my summer sister. I know that tomorrow I'll wake up and everything will be back to normal.

I hope.

CHAPTER 20

FREE HUGS—ALL YOU HAVE TO DO IS ASK

We didn't catch much on *My Way* today. And there were no light-house photo ops, either. Instead, it was drizzly and windy, and the choppy water tossed us around like rag dolls. The couple on board wasn't having any fun, and neither was I. It wasn't because of the weather, though. When I saw Linc before I left this morning, he was in a foul mood because his search had turned up empty, and of course my fight with Poppy weighed on my shoulders like an overstuffed backpack.

"Bea, I'm home." I kick off my wet sneakers and peel the plastic rain poncho from my body. The house feels clammy and smells extra musty.

I find her in the kitchen leaning against the sink with her eyes closed and face pinched.

She blinks rapidly like she's waking up from a deep sleep. The flimsy skin under her eyes sags more than usual. It takes a few seconds before her face relaxes into its normal shape.

Nervous prickles grip the back of my neck. "Are you okay?"

Bea picks up a dish towel and wipes the countertop like nothing happened. "Must have stood up too quickly. A case of the woozies is all. Where are you going?"

"Nowhere." I glance at my damp clothes. "I've been out fishing with Captain Holbrook, remember?"

Her forehead wrinkles. "Of course, I do. What I meant was how was it? You look miserably cold."

"Now that you mention it," I say as the words *must have hot chocolate* seize my brain. I open the door to the panty and grab the box, but it's empty of packets. Drat. As I search for something else to eat, I notice things in there that shouldn't be: an old rotary phone, a 1999 calendar, a bouquet of silk flowers marked with a red sticker—50 percent off.

I close the door quickly.

"There's nothing to eat around here." I clutch my stomach for dramatic effect.

Bea squeezes the bridge of her nose before she rolls the towel into a ball and throws it on the counter. "You're right, I can't even keep the cupboard full."

I rush to her. "I didn't mean it like that."

She dabs at her eyes. "I'm sorry. I wish everything were the same, but it's not. This is probably the worst visit you've ever had."

Seeing her like this makes me want to start bawling. I don't like when grown-ups cry. It's scary. I wrap my arms around her and she hugs me back.

"I'll make it up to you," she says into my matted hair.

I wish away that familiar sting in my eyes and will myself to keep it together. If we both start blubbering, I don't know what we'll do.

A buzzing sound startles us apart. Bea hurries to her purse. "It's my timer. Supposed to remind me to take my pills, but it's only reminding me how much I hate that thing." She turns it off and returns with a welcome surprise found in her magic bag: two packets of hot chocolate.

We take our drinks to the deck now that the sky has been scrubbed clean of all evidence of rain. A bright sun warms my outsides while the sweet liquid soothes me inside. Bea waves to a neighbor chugging by on his rugged skiff while seagulls circle overhead until they find an appealing perch—a chimney, rooftop, or the rocks below. Out here, I feel calmer. Maybe Linc's got a point with that tent of his. Things are getting too weird inside this house.

"Hey, Bea, remember last summer when you took Poppy and me to Little Moose Cove and the three of us created our own Olympic games?"

The corners of her mouth turn up. "What was it— swimming, obstacle course . . ."

I finish her sentence, "and best shell collection."

"Which I won."

"Naturally," I say, grinning. "Mom was convinced we were lost at sea since we were gone all afternoon, but it was so fun."

She smiles and sips her drink. "A good memory, indeed."

"I was hoping we could go again this summer, but . . . I doubt anyone's got the time."

Bea grips her mug with both hands and stares at the spot in the cove where Grandpa used to moor his boat. "Tell you what—we'll make time."

"Really? That would be awesome."

"Let me know which days are good for you and Poppy, and we'll figure it out."

A pang hits me deep inside. "Yeah, about that, we're not speaking at the moment."

She looks surprised. "Well, whatever it is, I'm sure it's fixable. I can't imagine you two staying mad for long. You should call her."

Thinking about calling Poppy makes me queasy, but maybe Bea's right. "Fine. I'll do it when she gets back from work."

"She's at Quayle's? Perfect. Let's go."

"Now?"

"You said it yourself: we need food." She gives my hand a squeeze. "I'm sure you and Poppy will patch things up. It's never a good idea to let a little tiff fester into something bigger. You need to let it go."

Funny, coming from the lady who can't let go of anything, but I'll take her advice and leave it at that.

CHAPTER 21

WHEN IN DOUBT ... MUMBLE

Bea grabs a shopping cart and steers it to the produce section. Into the basket I toss potatoes, celery, and onions, ingredients for her famous haddock chowder. Then she heads to the fish counter and instructs me to get bread from the bakery section. On my way, I pass Poppy's sister at the register, her nose buried in a book.

"Hi, Mona."

She looks up. "Hey," she says with the enthusiasm of a depressed penguin.

My eyes wander to a bulletin board tacked with local flyers.

QUILT SHOW SEPTEMBER 1ST.

BEAN HOLE SUPPER NEXT TUESDAY.

YARD SALE: 12 PERCY LANE, EVERYTHING MUST GO!

"Can I help you?" she asks.

Caught off guard, I stammer, "Uh . . . got a pen?"

She hands me a blue ballpoint, and I scribble *Percy Lane* on my palm.

"Is Poppy here?"

Her eyes lower back to her book. "She better be."

I return the pen. "It's no big deal. My grandma and I are just buying stuff."

Ugh, sometimes I say the dumbest things.

When I find Poppy, she's squatting in front of the frozen food case, spritzing it with glass cleaner and wiping it down.

She flinches a little when she sees me.

"Didn't mean to scare you." I chew on my lip.

"Let's go somewhere private." She grabs my hand and leads me through the swinging double doors to the back room, a cramped mess of food crates, hot ovens, and Mr. Quayle's paper-strewn desk. (Kind of like Bea's place but with yummy smells.) We lean against a floury work surface where a sheet of oatmeal raisin cookies cool. Poppy removes one with a spatula and hands it to me.

It's a peace offering, and I accept it. I gobble the cookie in two bites, savoring the mix of crunch and syrupy sweetness.

She helps herself to one, and we chew in silence for a few minutes. I don't know where to begin. I probably shouldn't have left the Ferris wheel. But she shouldn't have tossed me aside like a taco wrapper.

"Sorry," we blurt at the same time.

She flashes a crooked grin and gives me a second cookie. "That was so messed up."

I'm not sure if she's talking about the fair or how we both said sorry together.

"That was the worst night," I say. "You were so mad."

"So were you."

"I wasn't mad at you, but I was really annoyed. Can you blame me? As soon as you saw him, you basically forgot I existed."

She twirls a wisp of hair around her finger. "I didn't do it on purpose, I swear. You don't understand. He was paying attention to me. It's rare when someone pays attention to just me. It, like, never happens."

I pay attention to you, I want to scream. Why don't I count?

She looks at me all concerned. "Wait a minute, you don't like Gio, right? I mean, I asked you about a million times and you always said no. Is that what this is about?"

I groan. "No, Poppy, that's not it at all."

"Then, what *is* it about?"

How do I start? *It's about the fact that everything feels different this summer. That you're supposed to be my best friend, but now it sometimes feels awkward to be in the same room; that all our traditions now fall under the category of babyish; that you'd rather spend time with a guy who used to call you Poopy.*

I take a deep breath. "We need some me-and-you time, don't you think? No distractions. No drama. I was talking to

Bea, and she said she could take us to Little Moose Cove again. I totally want to go, but . . . do you?"

Poppy slides the rest of the cookies onto a plastic tray while I brace myself for *I'm too busy* or *No, thanks.*

"That sounds like a perfect idea," she finally says. "You're right. No distractions."

Having her agree is the best thing that has happened to me all day.

"I'll need to clear it with my dad, though, and probably Leanne, too."

"No problem. You tell me when and we'll do it."

She breathes a sigh of relief. "You're the best." She sticks out her arm and shakes her friendship bracelet. Unraveled threads stick up everywhere. "See? A little frayed, but still together. Just like us."

CHAPTER 22

WHAT HAPPENS AT GRANDMA'S STAYS AT GRANDMA'S

I turn the dial on the portable radio until I find a song that both Bea and I can agree on. The Beatles' "Here Comes the Sun" wins and becomes the soundtrack for our cooking session.

Singing at the top of her lungs, Bea slices the white fillets into large chunks while I chop carrots, celery, and onions and add them to the soup pot. Before long, the contents of the haddock chowder are simmering and the kitchen smells brackish from the boiled fish. Another song plays on the radio; one I've never heard of but has a faster beat. Bea cranks up the music and grabs my hands for an impromptu dance-a-thon. She tries to teach me a dance called the Lindy Hop, which is a lot of spinning and turning and some pretty fancy footwork, especially for a grandma. I step on her toes a couple times, but she doesn't seem to mind. I'm about to show her some moves from my generation when she sees the time on the kitchen wall clock. She bolts to the family room, informing me that

Antiques Roadshow started five minutes ago and she doesn't want to miss a second more.

I remove the KISS THE COOK apron she lent me and join her in front of the TV. Together we watch a man from Texas wait to find out if his Babe Ruth–autographed baseball is worth a gazillion dollars. Right when the expert in the spiffy blue suit is about to reveal the price, a shrill *BRRRRINGGG* steps on his words. Bea shoots the telephone a dirty look and makes no effort to answer it.

I grab the phone, hoping to hear from Poppy. Mom lays into me without even a hello.

"Why didn't you tell me?" she says.

The sharp edge in her voice makes me wince. "Tell you what?"

"About what happened at the flea market. Or should I say what didn't happen."

"Hold on." I take the phone onto the deck and slide the door behind me. The curly cord stretches behind me like a tight leash. "I didn't say anything because I knew you'd get upset, which you are. Who told you, anyway?"

"Not that it matters, but Ray. He said she wouldn't sell anything and you guys were the only ones who left with a full carload of stuff."

"Well, Ray is a total spying jerk!"

"That's not the point, Shayne," Mom snaps. "I don't think you realize how bad the situation has gotten."

"Of course I do. I'm living in it every single day!" My blood simmers like the chowder. Why does she have to stick her nose into everything? If that stupid flea market was so important to her, then she should have come up here and dealt with it herself.

Mom's silence makes my whole body tense with that feeling of dread you get when you know something horrible is coming.

"Bea is in serious financial trouble," she finally blurts.

Through the glass, I steal a glance at my grandmother, her eyes glued to the TV.

"After Grandpa died, I knew it wasn't going to be easy," Mom says. "He left her some life insurance money, but not a lot. About six months ago, Bea and I opened a joint bank account so I could deposit money to help her out. But after a while, I noticed she kept withdrawing cash but wasn't paying her bills."

"What was she doing with the money?" I ask.

"What do you think?" she says, her voice thick with sarcasm. "Thrift shops, yard sales, flea markets. She has an addiction and it's getting out of hand. I know how she is, buying a trinket here and there. 'It's only fifty cents,' she'll say. But it adds up, trust me. Before you know it, the house is overstuffed with things you don't need and there's no food in the pantry."

I bite my tongue, determined not to blab what I saw earlier today.

Mom continues. "Honestly, I was thrilled when she went back to work, and when she said she was cleaning out her house, I thought, *finally* she has come to her senses. But according to the bank, she hasn't paid her mortgage in two months."

I press my hand to my forehead to rub out an oncoming headache. What would I know about mortgages? That's grown-up stuff, not something to talk about with your twelve-year-old daughter.

"She didn't seem worried when we went to Quayle's. She even let me buy chocolate and marshmallows to make s'mores later," I say.

My mom sighs. "I'm sorry. You don't belong in the middle of this. It was a mistake to think you could handle this alone. Honey, I think I need to come up there."

I picture my mom stepping through the front door, her hand flying to her mouth in total disbelief. First, she'll yell at Bea. Then at me. She'll say I wasn't honest with her and yank me out of here faster than one of her gray hairs. Even though I don't like what's going on, I'm not ready for that either. "If you come, you and Bea will only fight and everyone will be miserable. Besides, Bea and I have a new plan."

"What kind of plan?" she asks.

I glance at the note I jotted on my hand. *Everything must go!*

"The flea market was too overwhelming for Bea, so we were thinking about having our own private yard sale." The lie comes out fast. I only hope I can turn it into a truth.

"I appreciate it, Shayne, I really do, but at this point I doubt that's going to be enough—"

I cut in. "Wait, there's more. I may have found something at the flea market that could be worth a lot of money."

"Good God, you sound just like her."

"Listen, they're ancient bullets, one hundred and fifty years old. I have a reputable source who says they could be the real deal."

Her groan is long and tired. "Look. I don't have time for fantasies right now. The bottom line is we don't have the money to support her outright. If she can't make some big changes then . . . I don't know . . . she might have to sell her house and move in with us."

The thought is so ridiculous I have to snort. "She'll never do that. You two wouldn't survive the first week."

"She may not have a choice."

I can't believe what I'm hearing. Sell Bea's house? Move in with us?

Is this my last summer in Maine?

CHAPTER 23

I'M NOT BOSSY, I JUST HAVE GOOD IDEAS

After that phone call, I knew I had to get to the Soldier & Saber stat. For two days straight, I nag Linc, who in turn nags Cranky, and between the two of us Cranky finally agrees to drive us there, probably just to shut us up.

There's a sticker on the door of the antique store that says TOP-RATED SELLER. I feel encouraged; this place is legit. We step inside. Military weapons, uniforms, flags, and other collectibles crowd the tiny space. I corner the shopkeeper, an old man with distractingly long eyebrow hairs, and ask him if he would appraise my five bullets.

From the bunch, Mr. Eyebrows grasps a rounded pewter one between his stubby fingers and lifts it to the light. "This looks like it came from a .30 caliber handgun," he says, "probably an officer's weapon."

I stare at him with a straight face. Something tells me it's best if you don't show emotion. I try to catch Linc's eye, but he's too busy drooling over the display of pins and buttons in the case beneath us. Cranky examines the rifles stacked neatly against the wall. I drum my fingers on the counter.

Mr. Eyebrows selects another bullet from my collection. "This one was dug up. You can still see the mud caked in the grooves. Most likely came from a Springfield rifle."

"So . . . are they worth anything?" I can barely breathe.

He jiggles them in his hand. The entire room seems to pause for this very moment, almost like the earth has stopped spinning. I watch for his lips to form words. It doesn't have to be the biggest number ever, just enough to cover Bea's bills, to get her out of trouble, to allow me to keep coming back to Maine.

The man flashes a kind, yellow-toothed smile. "I'll tell you what. How about I give you one dollar for all of them."

One dollar? I feel dizzy. "Are you sure? That lady made it sound like they were worth a lot of money. They belonged to her dead husband's collection."

He makes a clucking sound with his tongue. "I'm sorry to be the bearer of bad news, sweetheart, but people buy things from here all the time, hoping to turn a profit. The dead husband stuff makes for an interesting story, though."

"But . . . but . . ." I stammer. "What a liar!"

Mr. Eyebrows shakes his head as he hands me back my bullets. "Truth is you can find these all over battlefields. I know people who spend their Sunday mornings searching for them with a metal detector and a plastic cup." He reaches into a cabinet behind him and pulls out a silver bowl. "See?"

I peer inside. Hundreds of Civil War bullets exactly like the ones I have.

"Go ahead, take one," he says like he's offering me a mint.

Linc and I loiter at the store's exit while we wait for Cranky to decide which hunting knife he wants to buy. I feel like we're never going to get out of here.

"Look on the bright side," Linc says. "You're the proud owner of a piece of history. Cool, right?"

My teeth sink into my lower lip as I glower at Linc. "Be quiet. Some expert you are."

"Hey, don't take it out on me. This was your big idea." He lowers his voice. "Anyhow, you're the lucky one. It's not like you *lost* something precious, like the family heirloom that your grandfather risked his life to save. If anyone should be in a bad mood, it's me."

Linc's ranting doesn't make me feel any better. In fact, I feel worse. Make that *worthless*, like those bullets. Serves me right for believing my own daydream, thinking I could put on a superhero cape and swoop into town to save the day.

"Whoa," Linc says as he hurries over to a nearby display case. "Shayne, look. It's another Medal of Honor."

"It's a replica," Mr. Eyebrows says as he cleans his glasses with the end of his flannel shirt. "Twenty dollars if you want it. You're not going to find the real thing in here. It's illegal to sell them, even wear them, if you weren't the recipient."

Linc's eyes flutter and he sways ever so slightly. No way I can catch him if he faints.

As soon as Mr. Eyebrows leaves us to help another customer, Linc unravels. "Did you hear what he said? I wasn't supposed to wear it. Now I'm doubly doomed!"

"You're not doomed. You didn't know, and I won't tell anyone."

"It doesn't matter, anyway, because it's gone," he says through his teeth. "It's only a matter of time before Grandpa asks for the medal back. My best hope is that he's forgotten about it. You know, out of sight, out of mind."

Out of sight, out of mind.

Ideas pour into my brain faster than a raging river. While Linc paces and mutters to himself, my fingers curl around my bargain basement bullets. Maybe Bea can't part with anything because it's too painful to watch it go. But if she doesn't see it go, maybe she won't know it's not there.

I grip Linc's arm. "I have an idea that may help us both. What if we had a secret yard sale while Bea's at work? I'll sell all the things she couldn't part with at the Cedar Island Flea Market, plus I can sell my bracelets, too." I stick my arm in his face to show him my handiwork. "I've already made a bunch of these, but I can crank out a ton more fast. What do you think?"

Linc scrunches his face. "I think I'm totally confused. How is this supposed to help me?"

"Twenty dollars," I say.

"Huh?"

I crook a finger for him to lean in close. "That's your cut if you help me pull this off. For twenty dollars, you could buy a certain something here at the Soldier & Saber to replace that other certain something you can't find."

His eyes bug out. "Ohhhhh. Right. Count me in."

My body tingles with renewed energy. "There's one last piece to this puzzle. We need to get the word out."

Linc looks doubtful. "How are we going to do that?"

"I have connections." I puff a flyaway curl out of my face. Whether she'll say yes, though, is another story.

CHAPTER 24

DREAM BIG OR GO HOME

Poppy studies my homemade flyer: THOMAS COVE YARD SALE! THIS SATURDAY. EVERYTHING MUST GO! My heart jackhammers my rib cage while she scans it. Did I go overboard with the rainbow colors and bubble letters? She probably thinks it's stupid.

Poppy glances up. "What happened? No takers at the flea market?"

"Not exactly. She had trouble letting go of her things, so I thought if I ran a yard sale for her while she's at work, she wouldn't have to watch other people take her stuff. Anyway, I was wondering if you could post my flyer on the bulletin board at Quayle's."

Poppy crinkles her nose. "I don't know if I'm allowed. Honestly, if we hung up every yard sale flyer around town, it would wallpaper our entire store."

"But you post them all the time!"

"My dad does it as a favor for some of his friends."

"Then tell him you're doing a favor for me. Please?" I clasp my hands together. "You don't understand. I need to get the word out. My mom's going crazy. She thinks Bea has an addiction, and she might, but that's not the point. If I don't get rid of at least some of the junk in her house, then Mom will blame Bea and won't let me come back next summer."

"Seriously? That's harsh."

"Tell me about it."

"And Bea's okay with all this?" she asks.

I sip my water and shake my head. "She doesn't know, but trust me, this is the only way it's going to work."

Poppy rolls up the flyer and sticks it in her backpack. "I'll ask Leanne if it's okay."

I breathe a sigh of relief. "Awesome, thanks."

Katie approaches our table with a large tray balanced on her shoulder. My mouth salivates at the glorious sight of lobster chunks spilling out the top of toasted buns, crispy onion rings fried to perfection, and thick vanilla shakes.

"Enjoy your lunch, ladies," Katie sings, her perfect ponytail swishing behind her.

Poppy cracks her gum and steals a peek at the swinging double doors that lead to the kitchen. I already told her that Bea said Gio wasn't working today, but she keeps glancing anyway like he'll magically appear.

I dive into my lobster roll. *Mmmmm.* Heaven on a bun.

Poppy pulls her hair back to keep it from falling in her food and reveals a shiny gold cuff at the top of her right ear.

"When did you get that?" I say with my mouth full.

Her hand floats up to touch it. "Do you like it? I pierced it last night—I mean, my friend did it for me. You don't know her, she goes to my school."

A pang of jealously pricks my gut. "Last night? Why didn't you call me?"

Before she can answer, a hefty swig of milkshake rewards her with brain freeze. While she massages her forehead to make the icy pain go away, I make a snap decision not to bug her about not calling me. She already said she'd post my flyer; I don't want anything to ruin our lunch together.

"So, did you ask your dad yet about Little Moose Cove?"

"Darn, I forgot," she says.

"C'mon, Poppy, ask him already. We don't have much time left. I'm leaving next week."

"Quit pressuring me."

My head jerks back. "I'm not pressuring you."

"Yes, you are. You may be here on vacation, but if you haven't noticed, I'm not. Leanne loads me up with hours at the market like I'm her personal slave. If I complain, she tells my parents, and they say if I don't contribute to the family business then they'll take away my phone. My life sucks rocks."

"No, it doesn't."

"It does." She sulks at her sandwich. "They don't care about me. I could be covered in flesh-eating insects and have blood coming out of my eyes, and they'd still insist that I sweep aisle four."

"Thanks for the tasty visual."

"I'm not kidding. It's not like I have a choice about it. Look at Leanne. Dad made her manager this summer. It's like he's digging in his hooks so she can't leave." She pushes her plate away. Her shoulders slump as she stares off into space. "Face it. I'm stuck here forever."

The onion rings leave my lips slick with grease. "Stuck here?" I am dumbfounded. "Are you kidding me? You're the lucky one. I beg my parents all the time to visit more often. I'd live here year-round if I could. To me, Thomas Cove is one of the best places on the planet, not somewhere you get stuck."

A hint of a smile appears on her face, making me feel encouraged.

"That's why you need to go to Little Moose," I say. "You need a break. We can lie on the beach all day and do nothing. I'll bring plenty of Bea's gossip magazines."

"As long as they're from the twenty-first century," she says. We both crack up.

I settle back in my seat, completely stuffed, satisfied, and happy that I brought Poppy back from spiraling into a wicked bad mood.

☆

After lunch, we browse the café's gift shop. The air smells of vanilla and cinnamon from the scented candles for sale.

The cashier looks up from her crossword puzzle. "Poppy, tell your father his milk prices are too high. They're fifty cents more than Straw's."

"Not my problem," Poppy says under her breath as we browse the made-in-Maine products like maple syrup, honey, and blueberry jam.

I pick up a starfish magnet and gape at the price tag. "Ten dollars for this?"

Poppy whispers. "You could totally walk out of here with that and she'd never know. She's completely out of it."

I glance over my shoulder at the cashier bent over her puzzle. "I don't want it that bad." My heartbeat speeds up as I throw the magnet back into the bin. The blank look on Poppy's face makes me unsure if she was joking.

We walk to a wall of T-shirts and pick through the stacks. I pull out a bright red one with a #1 GRANDMA decal in pink and white on the front.

"Hey, do you think I should get this for Bea? It's so tacky, she'd love it."

Poppy's eyebrows rise. "I don't think you should be buying Bea anything."

My cheeks warm as I throw the shirt back on the shelf. "I'm kidding."

Poppy riffles through the earring racks. She holds different pairs up to her new piercing and admires the look in the warped mirror pasted onto the side. She shows me miniature dolphins dangling by a silver chain. "Cute or lame?" she asks.

"Definitely cute."

I run my fingers through the necklaces that hang from wooden pegs. A double necklace with a pink BFF heart cut down the middle catches my eye. I could wear one half and Poppy could wear the other. But would she?

I hold it up for her to see. "Cute or lame?"

Instead of answering, Poppy grabs my elbow and yanks me toward the exit. "We need to leave."

"Why?"

"Now," she says through her teeth.

Outside, Poppy slips her arms through the strings of her backpack, eyeing the entrance to the gift shop. I cross my arms. "What was that all about?"

She won't look at me. "Nothing. I'm just bored. I don't like the food, and the gift shop is stupid. So, if you don't mind, I'd like to do something that's fun and not horrible."

She hops on her bike and fastens her helmet. "Let's go."

As we pedal back to her house, my stomach begins to hurt. Since when did the Cod Café become the world's most awful place? What began as a totally yummy lunch has left me with the worst taste in my mouth.

CHAPTER 25

IF AT FIRST YOU DON'T SUCCEED . . . RUN

THOMAS COVE YARD SALE! EVERYTHING MUST GO! The large cardboard sign sits at the entrance to Thomas Cove with an arrow pointing toward Bea's house. With less than forty-eight hours to make it happen, I can't believe my secret yard sale might actually work.

As soon as Bea left for work this morning and Cranky had headed out for a day of fishing, Linc and I hustled all the boxes and bags of stuff intended for the Cedar Island Flea Market to the end of Bea's driveway. We helped ourselves to Cranky's fold-up card table and brought along Linc's tartan blanket from his tent. I lined up all the goods with their price tags facing outward for easy access and transparency. No switching prices or other sneaky moves here. This stuff has to go fast.

I wish I didn't have to hide the yard sale from Bea, but it's really for the best. Out of sight, out of mind, like Linc said.

Once I set up the sign on the side of the road, it didn't take long before customers appeared. The candlesticks were snapped up first, followed quickly by a stack of old dishes, a couple comic books, and some unused hand lotions. Linc worked the cashbox while I greeted customers and showed off the merchandise. I wondered if all this traffic meant that Poppy had posted my sign. I hoped she had. That would mean the world to me.

"Do you have any dress-up clothes?" asks a large woman with ruddy cheeks. "My daughter works at the preschool and they're always in need of these things."

I skip over to the clothing section and hand the woman a plastic diamond tiara. "Would something like this work?"

"Perfect," she says. "How much?"

"One dollar." I motion to Linc. "The cashier will check you out."

As soon as he holds out his hand to receive the money, the screeching sound of slammed brakes makes us all flinch. Bea hurls herself out of the driver's seat with her Cod Café apron still tied around her waist.

My heart practically arrests on the spot. "What are you doing here?" I ask in a shaky voice.

Linc bolts out of his seat and takes off in the opposite direction, cutting across Cranky's lawn until he disappears into the folds of his tent. "Traitor," I mutter as Bea staggers toward me.

She breathes noisily out of her nose like an angry bull; a beaded necklace dangles from her clutched fist. "How could you?"

"Let me explain," I say.

"How do you think I felt when one of my customers came in wearing *my* necklace? I asked her where she got it and she says she picked it up at a yard sale on Thomas Cove!"

The woman who bought the tiara tiptoes between us. "Bea, your granddaughter is doing such a great job."

"Stay out of it, Martha," Bea snaps. "And give that back."

A bewildered look clouds Martha's face, but she doesn't hand it over. "Diane could really use this in her classroom. Twenty preschoolers, and of course there's barely any money for supplies."

Martha's calm voice only inflames Bea more. She grips the tiara so hard that her knuckles turn ghostly white. "It's. Mine!"

"Bea, let go!" I scream as the ladies tug at it.

Martha finally relinquishes the fake crown with disgust. "Honestly! What has gotten into you?"

Bea yells at Martha's back as she walks away. "It's not for sale! There's nothing to buy here!" She points at a man hovering by a worn lampshade. "That goes for you, too."

He holds up his hands like he's under arrest. "I didn't touch anything."

Bea swivels her head at the sound of a car's engine turning, and she dashes after it. "Don't leave! What do you have?"

The friendly air that surrounded my yard sale has curdled like sour milk. Parents grab their children's hands and hurry them off the property. Bea darts from car to car like an anxious chicken loose from its pen. Some customers manage to escape, their tires spitting gravel as they peel out.

Bea's apron unties and falls to the ground. Coins roll out from one of the pockets. I hurry beside her to help recover the scattered change as she drops to her knees and buries her face in her hands.

Hot, embarrassed tears slide down my cheeks. "I'm sorry. I was only trying to help."

Bea picks herself off the ground. Grass stains and bits of dirt cover her khaki pants. "I *never* said you could do this."

I want to be brave and look Bea in the eye, but her steely voice makes my gaze slip.

She reties the apron and smooths her hands over the front pockets. "If you really want to help, really and truly, then you'll put everything back where you found it."

My shoulders droop as we silently pack up everything. Again.

Bea picks up a worn cardboard box filled with clothes. An unwashed smell rises out of it like steam. "I'm not something to tidy up like a closet, for heaven's sake. I don't understand you. These are your grandpa's things. What if you want them someday?"

A chill tickles my spine. What on earth would I do with his old clothes?

"I won't." I brush the wetness off my face. "I don't understand. You said you were going to get rid of it all. That was the plan. That's why I'm here!"

Bea steps toward her house with the box weighing heavily in her arms. "You can't rush me. It's a slow process going through everything. What if I find something valuable?"

"But we're running out of time! What if you have to move?"

A sudden coughing fit erupts from her chest. She doubles over, causing the box to tip. Wrinkled shirts, ripped pants, and scuffed shoes spill onto the ground. Her hand flutters to her chest. "I'm not moving," she says in a raspy voice. "What did your mother say, exactly?"

"Nothing," I lie, "but you're buying so much stuff, and it's piling up, and it scares me."

Bea pokes a finger in my face. "You sound like her. Sticking your nose somewhere it shouldn't be. From now on, new rules: you're not allowed to touch any of my treasures."

She moves to Linc's tartan blanket and grabs each end. The contents clink and clank and crash as she gathers up the corners to create one humongous hobo sack. "Do you hear me, Shayne Whittaker? Any of it!"

I follow her into the house, leaving the litter of Grandpa's strewn clothes behind. The sack thuds behind her as she clomps up the stairs. "That's Linc's blanket. I need to give it back." I bound up the steps two at a time to catch her. When I reach the top, I freeze.

Bea's bedroom door is left wide open, and, for the first time in years, I see inside. Wall-to-wall piles of stuff, waist-high, with only a narrow path carved out to her unmade bed. Everything's jumbled together, an unopened package of toilet paper mixed in with a sweater and an umbrella and a lampshade. Toaster ovens on top of newspapers on top of high-heeled shoes—it's like a dump truck overturned and left the scene for good.

I gape at the sheer amount of it all—so much that it makes Junk Mountain look like a speed bump. I want to throw up. I want to go home. A couple of the mounds are as tall as me. Everything is packed in tight. I bet I could climb to the top and not fall through.

Bea stands near the bed, her back to me. Then she turns slowly like she knows she's being watched. Our eyes meet and her expression changes rapidly: from mad, to sad, to embarrassed.

"Leave me alone!"

The door slams shut in my face.

CHAPTER 26

IF YOU MET MY FAMILY YOU'D UNDERSTAND

We're supposed to go to Little Moose Cove today, but sitting patiently in the *Knot for Sale* falls under the category of wishful thinking. Bea hasn't said a word to me since yesterday's debacle, but I'm hoping she'll show up anyway, and we can pretend that none of this ever happened.

Bea has never been this furious with me. Ever. Even when she gets annoyed, she always bounces back quickly. It appears that now we've reached a new level. What happened to her "impossibly half full" glass? Am I the one who emptied it?

I barely slept last night. Images of Bea's bedroom kept floating into my dreams. I can't believe she would rather hang on to other people's junk and smelly clothes than keep her house. Than take care of me. Mom said Bea has an addiction, and she's right: it's called hoarding. I've seen those TV shows about hoarders who can never throw anything out until they're practically buried in moldy garbage piled to the ceiling. It creeps me out. Is that where Bea is headed?

Linc lumbers down the ramp with a backpack slung over his shoulder. Even though Poppy couldn't come (more like never asked her dad and I got tired of reminding her), I'm glad Linc agreed to join me. He's become like a favorite pair of pajamas: completely comfy. Besides, I don't want to be alone with Bea. I wouldn't know what to say to her.

"Filled up with seasickness meds and good to go," he says, all eager beaver.

I glance up at the house. "Don't hold your breath. She hasn't come out of her room since yesterday."

He winces. "That bad, huh."

"Worse."

Linc hops in the boat and sits next to me. White smears of sunblock on his cheeks beg to be rubbed in.

I really want to tell him what I saw, how sick it made me feel, how scared, too. But what will he think of me living in a house like that? I can't believe I used to think *he* was weird. We're the real freaks around here.

"So . . . what should we do now?" he asks.

"Keep waiting, I guess." I prop my elbows on the hard ledge, cross my feet, and inspect the chipped blue polish on my toes.

A sense comes over me that I'm being watched. I lift my head to find Linc's eyes resting on my turquoise bikini top. I feel my cheeks turning pink.

He smacks my shoulder.

"Hey!"

"Got it." He flips his palm to show me the smashed mosquito.

I switch to the captain's chair to reclaim some personal space. Linc pulls a thick book out of his backpack.

"Hope you don't mind if I read while we wait," he says, holding it up for me to see the cover: *Chancellorsville 1863: The Souls of the Brave.*

I snort. "Is that your idea of a beach read?"

"It's actually one of the best accounts I've ever read. Do you want me to tell you what it's about?"

"Sure," I say, closing my eyes. "I could use a good nap."

"Very funny."

I keep my eyes shut. It feels too good. Lapping waves and the boat's rhythmic bobbing soothe me like a lullaby. Next thing I know, Linc shakes my shoulder.

"Shayne, wake up. She's coming."

I wipe off a thread of drool with the back of my hand as Bea sweeps down the ramp, beach-ready in a flowing cover-up, floppy hat, and dark sunglasses. How she can find anything in that room is beyond me. She'd actually look completely normal if it weren't for the multiple bags she carries in each hand. Is she bringing all her junk with her to the beach? Wonderful.

Linc rushes to his feet. "Let me help you with those." He grabs the bags and sticks them next to me, a cruel reminder of my colossal failure yesterday.

Bea places her hand over her heart and looks at him with admiration. "Such a nice young man, so polite. I bet you don't give your grandfather *any* grief."

"Okayyyy, let's go," I say, trying to ignore that remark. No way I'm getting into another fight in front of Linc.

Her eyebrows knit into a frown behind her sunglasses. "Wait a minute, I'd like to give a present to our guest."

I slump back in my seat with a groan.

She clears her throat and turns her attention to Linc. "Shayne tells me you're some kind of Civil War expert."

He blushes. "I don't know about that."

Bea rummages through a canvas tote. "Now, I don't know if you already have one of these but . . . here."

Linc examines his gift: a coffee mug with a picture of the Union army general William Tecumseh Sherman on the front. Underneath there's a caption that says WAR IS HELL.

I roll my eyes.

Linc's face lights up. "Awesome, thanks!"

"You're welcome." Bea lifts her sunglasses and peers at me with triumph in her eyes. "See, I don't have a problem relinquishing my things. At least somebody appreciates my treasures even if *you* think it's all trash."

CHAPTER 27

A WALK ON THE BEACH IS GOOD FOR THE SOUL

A salty spray cools me as the *Knot for Sale* cuts through the water. It feels refreshing, like a power wash of all the yuck I've felt and seen. Bea chats up Linc the whole ride, telling him how the property that surrounds Little Moose Cove belongs to Mr. Utterback, one of her old regulars at the Cod Café. I've met him once or twice before, but he travels a lot so there's a good chance we'll have the cove all to ourselves.

Ten minutes later, Bea steers into a quiet sandy alcove framed by rows of thick pine trees. She pulls alongside a lone floating dock, and I hop out to help moor the boat. She throws me a line with a big loop tied at the end, which I slip over a thick post. Wooden planks, many blackened with rot, creak under my feet.

We grab our gear and set up camp on the coffee-colored sand. Bea spreads out towels while I help Linc with the beach umbrella. The sky is a swatch of blue, so clear and bright it's as if it were scrubbed and polished to a shine. I bask in the sun's warmth on my bare shoulders.

"Nice spot," Linc says as he surveys the scenery.

"You should see the backyard. It butts right up to the Atlantic Ocean." I pull on Linc's arm. "Come on, I'll show you."

"Will Mr. Utterback mind?" he asks Bea.

She waves him off. "I doubt he's even home, but he won't, I promise."

"Do you want to come with us?" I ask.

"No, thanks, I'll stay here and swim." She stretches a bright green rubber bathing cap over her head, and I have to look away. She reminds me of a turtle.

Linc and I cut up the short hill, which leads to a stone path. I cast a quick glance at the white clapboard cottage we pass on our right. With its drawn blinds, tall, uncut grass, and empty driveway, it looks like no one has been home in a long time.

We walk down a small slope to a wall of boulders that act as giant steps to the sea. Spreading our arms to keep our balance, we hop from one rock to the next. When we reach the water's edge, I sit on a flat ledge and enjoy the splash from the ocean's crashing waves.

"Shayne, check this out."

Linc points to a hermit crab a couple feet away. We lie side by side on our stomachs and watch its spindly legs grasp an empty speckled shell. The hermit crab pulls the new shell close, and, in a blink, hoists itself out of its old shell. Now, I've never seen a naked hermit crab before, and let me tell you, it is not pretty. Its body is an icky gray color and looks soft and slug-like. Thankfully, for everybody, it's only a quick second before the hermit crab drops itself into its new protective home.

As I rest my head on my hands, my thoughts drift to Bea. If only it were that simple, moving from house to house with nothing but a plunk. Truth is, I'm scared for her. What's going to happen when I leave? She shouldn't live by herself anymore. It's not safe. Would moving in with us really be so terrible?

I absentmindedly pick at the tiny pebbles that fill a crevice in the rock. Out tumbles a teeny orange shell, the color of a creamsicle. "It's so crazy the way Bea keeps everything. Even something like a ripped sock is off-limits. She's so obsessed with her stuff. I don't get it."

Linc props himself up on his elbows. "Yeah, I know. But look at me—you could say I'm obsessed about the Civil War. Maybe my reenactor gear is too much for some people, and I'd have more friends if I toned it down a bit. But you know what? I don't care. I like wearing the clothes, and studying battles, and thinking about my great-great-great-grandfather, keeping his memory alive. That's what makes me happy."

Something about what he says hits me. *Keeping memories alive.* Is that what Bea's doing? Living in the past? Is that why she hoards?

"Your obsession isn't hurting anybody, but Bea's isn't healthy and she could lose her house over it," I say.

He shrugs. "Maybe having all those things around her makes her feel good."

"I can understand why she would want to hold on to chicken-bird and other special things like that, but a box of moldy old clothes? Ew."

Linc sits up and crosses his legs. "It's funny how certain things can make you feel, though. Like, to you the Medal of Honor is just an antique, but to me it means so much more. When I hold it in my hand and close my eyes, it takes me to another time and place. I can be alongside Ogden Badger at Devil's Den, or I can be six years old again, when my dad took me to Virginia for my very first reenactment. The medal helps me remember. We used to visit my grandparents a lot in their old house in Belfast, and my grandma would take it out of this glass case and let me play with it all the time. No sneaking around or anything."

He jiggles a rock in his hand before chucking it into the sea. "Then she died, and then my parents got divorced, and we stopped visiting my grandpa for whatever reason, so . . . yeah. We used to be more together, not so broken into pieces like we are now."

I think about that. Is that how Bea feels with Grandpa

gone—broken into pieces? She has always been a collector, and I know her things hold great meaning, but now she's piling up stuff a million times over. It's like she's trying to fill a hole and never reaching the top. When will it stop?

"Change sucks," I blurt.

Linc wipes the grit from his hands as he stands. "Sometimes. But sometimes it can surprise you in a good way."

His blue eyes are honest and kind. He offers me a hand, and I take it. He lifts me to my feet, and together we walk back to the cove.

"So, what's your next move?" Linc asks.

In the distance, I see Bea sitting at the water's edge. "I'm going to call my mom and tell her everything. I can't handle this anymore."

"You tried. You did the best you could."

I offer him an awkward half grin. "Believe it or not, I've also decided to have another sale, but this time I'm only selling my bracelets. I've made so many, I don't know what to do with them. If I can raise at least twenty dollars, you can have it."

He looks surprised. "For what?"

"To buy that fake medal at the Soldier & Saber. You still haven't found the real one, and I don't want you to get in trouble."

"Thanks, but I have to tell him the truth." He lifts his chin and puffs out his chest. "If Second Lieutenant Ogden Badger can face the enemy and get his arm blown off, then I should be able to admit to Grandpa that I've lost the family's priceless heirloom. At least he won't take off my limbs." He looks down at them with a grimace. "I hope."

At the bottom of the hill, I spot Bea sitting on the sand, her legs splayed out in front of her in a funny way.

"Bea, what are you doing?" She doesn't move. I cup my hands around my mouth. "Bea!"

When we reach her, my heart nearly stops.

"I don't feel well," she says between coughing jags. Her face contorts with pain as she clutches her chest. I squat beside her as she unhooks the bathing cap's strap from under her chin.

"Should we call 9-1-1?" Linc's voice trembles as he kneels beside us.

Bea shakes her head. "I'll be fine. Just get me home."

Linc and I help her up, and I wrap a towel around her shoulders. She groans softly as we inch our way toward the dock.

"We're almost there," I say in a soothing voice. "A few more steps . . ."

The warped planks creak under our feet. Everything feels unstable now, a moment away from collapse. I instruct Linc to get in the boat first and together we help Bea climb in. Suddenly, she sinks to the floor and rests her head on the bench by the bow.

"I'm so dizzy," she says with a weak voice. "Shayne, you'll have to drive us back. Do you remember how?"

My pulse races. "I . . . I . . ."

Linc grabs the motor's handle and yanks the cord with a frantic sawing motion. "How do you start this thing?"

"Don't! Let me do it," I say, remembering what happened when I pulled the cord too fast. The last thing we need is a flooded engine.

We change seats. I take a deep breath, wrap my hand around the handle, and pull the cord with a firm, even movement.

"Come on, come on," I say through gritted teeth. The motor catches on the second try.

My legs and knees itch from baked-on sand. I lick my dry lips and order Linc to remove the dock lines. He does.

Check.

I shove the boat away from the dock with my foot like I've seen Bea do.

Check.

I throw the gear into drive. We're off.

"We're going home, Bea," I shout above the motor's whir.

The engine putters until I exit the cove. Then I let her rip, twisting the handle forward as far as it will go. We pick up speed. The roar of the engine competes with my racing heart.

Our beach towels flap in the wind as we bounce along the choppy seas. Linc holds Bea's hand. Her face looks sickly white.

The sun plays hide-and-seek behind fast-moving dark clouds. I scan the coastline for a lone fisherman, a house, anyone who can help us, but all I see are moored lobster boats and a blanket of evergreen forest. This better be the right direction. I can't get lost right now.

Stay calm, Shayne. Stay calm.

I shiver. Little puffs of damp, cool air swirl around me, and my skin breaks out in goose bumps. Finally, a waterfront home appears in a clearing. It looks fancy with its half-moon picture window and grand stone chimney. I ease up on the throttle. The motor calms to a bubbling purr, and the smell of boat fuel fills the air.

I cup my hands around my mouth. "Help! Help us! Hello!"

Linc joins in. "Anybody home? Please help us!"

Suddenly, the house vanishes before my eyes. In its place is nothing but a wall of white.

Oh, no. My blood turns to ice.

A thick cloud of fog rolls over the *Knot for Sale*. It swallows us whole.

CHAPTER 28

STAY ANCHORED

The fog is thick like pea soup. The only thing I can see clearly is the water below, flat and silvery green. Even Bea and Linc drift in and out of view. I keep thinking about what Cranky said about the dangers of fog. *What if we hit the rocks? What if a boat crashes into us? What if Bea dies?*

Bea lies on the floor of the boat with her eyes closed. Linc put a life vest under her head to use as a pillow and covered her with a beach towel.

He hugs his knees and rocks back and forth. "I wish I had my medal."

"It doesn't have special powers," I snap. I don't want to talk about this.

"But I feel stronger when it's with me," he says.

Honestly, I wish he had it, too. I could use some strength right about now. The dense air shrouds us like a cold, wet jacket. I briskly rub my legs to warm up. "What should I do?" I whisper to no one.

I check my phone, even though I never get good reception on the water. Today is no exception; I can't get a signal. Linc fiddles with switches on the marine radio. "How do you work this thing?"

"I don't know. Your grandpa wouldn't let us touch it unless it was an emergency."

"This qualifies, don't you think?" He stabs at the buttons. The number nine glows on the front digital display. Muffled sounds come from the speaker. Linc finds the volume knob and turns it up. It's a weather report.

"Give it to me." I lift the handheld microphone to my lips. "Help! Help!"

The weatherman drones on, something about a front coming in from the west.

"Try a different channel. There's got to be one for the coast guard," Linc says. "I can't remember which one Grandpa said it was."

I turn the dial a few times. "Help!" I say again.

Nothing but crackling static responds.

I can't stop thinking about my grandpa. I had cried in my mother's arms when the fog monster got him. But he'd sounded the horn to tell me everything was all right. I wish he were here, telling me the same thing right now.

He sounded the horn.

"Linc, move. I need to get under that bench."

He scooches out of the way, and I lift the cover to the storage bin. Under a heap of life jackets, I find a white canister with a bright orange megaphone on top, MARINE HORN written on the side.

I lift it over my head and press the button.

HWAAAAAAH.

The air horn's super-loud shrill practically blows out my ears. I glimpse at Bea. She moans softly.

I wait for something to happen: the sound of a passing boat, a faraway voice. Anything. All I hear is the squawk of gulls flying overhead.

"Try the radio again," Linc says.

I hold the microphone. "Help!"

"Say 'Mayday,'" he suggests.

"Mayday!"

"Say it three times. That's the universal distress call."

"Mayday! Mayday! Mayday!"

I switch channels. This time I hear a jumble of voices.

"Mayday! Mayday! Mayday!" I cry. "My grandmother has collapsed. Please help us."

"What's your position?" says a male voice.

My whole body trembles with nerves. "I don't know. We're on the *Knot for Sale* headed for Thomas Cove. We're in front of this really big house."

Linc taps my shoulder. "Tell him 43 north by 69 east."

I repeat the information to the invisible voice. Linc and I hold our breath as we wait for a response.

"How did you know that?" I whisper to him.

He holds up a crumpled nautical map. "It was in the bin. I'm kinda into coordinates if you haven't noticed."

The radio crackles with static.

Panic grips my throat. Did we lose him? Please, no!

A jolt catches us by surprise as the *Knot for Sale* rocks over a heavy wake.

Linc loses his footing and stumbles to the floor. "What's happening?" Pure fear strangles his voice.

Wakes come from boats. Boats in close range. But how can a boat see us in this fog? That's exactly what happened to my grandpa.

"Ohmigod, we're about to get hit!"

I yank Linc down to the floor of the boat and we brace ourselves for the impact.

As a last ditch effort, I lift the marine horn high in the air and press the button.

HWWWAHHH.

BURRRR-AHHHH.

A deep foghorn blast fills the air. Through airy wisps, I can make out the red painted hull of a lobster boat heading our way.

I gasp. "Captain Holbrook!" I stand and wave my arms over my head. "Over here!" My heart bursts with happiness. We're saved.

My Way sounds the horn again. Cranky sees us and waves back. He pulls up beside us and drops the anchor. "Throw me a rope," he says.

I toss him one of the dock lines. He grabs hold of it and pulls *Knot for Sale* closer to him. In one swift motion, he leaps into our boat, and it rocks under his weight. His face is crimson as he lifts Bea into his lap, her tiny frame dwarfed by his large size. He puts two fingers on the pulse in her neck.

She opens her eyes and two glassy orbs stare back, unfocused. She mumbles something that makes Cranky frown. "She's not making any sense. Shayne, sit with her and I'll drive you in."

"What about your boat?" I ask.

"I'll come back for it later."

The fog begins to thin as it lifts off the water. Cranky starts the engine. With him at the helm, a release takes over my body. I feel like I could sleep for a hundred days.

"How in the world did you find us?" I shout over the loud drone of the engine.

"Part luck," he replies. "I talked to Bea this morning, and she told me where you were going. It so happened I was pulling traps nearby, so when I heard your distress call and your coordinates, I knew exactly where you were. I already called the coast guard, and they've connected with the paramedics. Hang on, Bea, I'll get you home safely."

We barrel into the normally quiet Thomas Cove for our emergency landing. One angry kayaker shakes his fist at us since we're not supposed to be going this fast. In the distance, red lights flash, and what looks like the entire town waits for our arrival.

CHAPTER 29

NEVER GIVE UP

A paramedic listens to Bea's heartbeat with a stethoscope while another wraps a blood pressure cuff around her upper arm. Cranky huddles over them like a hulking quarterback. Linc and I stand at the top of the ramp to stay out of their way.

Behind me, I can feel a thousand eyes pressing into my back. On Thomas Cove, an ambulance pretty much equals the Super Bowl in excitement and viewership. Neighbors gather in clumps and whisper while they stare. Poppy emerges from one of the gossip pods and wedges herself between me and Linc.

"What happened?"

"Bea got sick while we were at Little Moose," I say.

"Oh," she says, surprised. "You went to Little Moose? I thought you and I were supposed to go."

I don't respond. I can't take my eyes off Bea lying on a stretcher, hooked up to an IV, some kind of clear fluid flowing from a plastic bag down a tube and into her arm.

The ramp sways from Cranky's heavy stride as he makes his way up to us. "They're taking her to the hospital, but I'll go with her. It's a good idea to have another adult around to answer questions," he says.

"Can I go, too?" I ask.

"Of course."

Poppy jumps in. "Maybe she should stay with me."

"Who's this?" Cranky asks me.

Poppy jams her hands on her hips while her mouth drops open, completely offended.

"She's my friend," I say.

Cranky breathes through his nose while he thinks about it. "That's probably a better idea." He hands me a pen and a tiny scrap of paper from his back pocket. "Write down your number, and I'll call you as soon as I know anything. Meanwhile, let your parents know Bea's at Down East Medical." He clamps a hand on Linc's shoulder. "Without those coordinates, it would have been very tough to find you. Good work, soldier."

Cranky rushes back to the paramedics, leaving Linc looking as red as a boiled lobster and Poppy as annoyed as a wet cat.

"Who does he think he is?" she says, arms crossed over

her chest. "*Who's this?* Like I'm some nobody. Shayne has only known me her whole life, you big jerk."

"Hey!" Linc snaps. "He's not a jerk. He actually rescued us on the water. If it wasn't for him, Bea could have died."

"Wait a second." Her eyes settle on me as she hooks a sharp thumb at Linc. "Are you saying you took *him* to Little Moose? I can't believe this."

Linc huffs. "It was a good thing I was there. Somebody needs to know how to read a nautical map for crying out loud."

Poppy smirks. "Well, a big congratulations to you. We should give this guy a *medal*, right, Shayne? You really deserve a medal." She slaps him on the back.

He jumps as if her hand were a piece of hot coal. "Get off me."

"Guys, stop it!" I shriek.

Murmurs ripple through the crowd as people stare at us fighting. Poppy glares at Linc, and I can tell she's unsure what her next move is. She settles on brushing imaginary dirt off her shoulder before drifting over to a group of rubberneckers; she's probably eager to trash Cranky, even though we just told her he saved Bea's life.

Linc rocks on his heels as he studies his feet. Finally, he looks up at me. "Did you tell her about the medal?"

"No."

He blinks fast. "I mean, we did swear that we'd keep each other's secrets. I kept yours, but I'm wondering if you blabbed mine."

"I didn't tell her, I swear."

"It's just . . ." He lets out a big breath. "I hope you weren't making fun of me, because it's not a joke. You should know that. I told you everything."

"Linc." I reach out to him, but he takes a step back.

"Listen, it's been a long day. I need to chill in my tent for a little while if you don't mind." He turns his back on me and walks away.

"Come on, Linc, come back."

It's no use. He pushes through the crowd until he can duck into the safety of his tent.

The paramedics roll the stretcher past me. Bea looks so old lying there with her eyes closed and a skinny oxygen tube under her nose. I brush my finger against her hand; her skin feels loose and clammy. Cranky follows behind, stopping to crush me in a bear hug.

"I won't leave her side," he says, lifting my chin to meet his gaze. "Don't worry."

I chew on my thumbnail as I watch the paramedics lift Bea into the back of the ambulance. When the double doors shut behind her, I lose it.

Poppy reappears just in time to slide an arm around my shoulders. "Don't cry. She'll be okay."

I'm sorry, Bea. I didn't mean to upset you. I am so, so sorry.

CHAPTER 30

I'M NOT HARD OF HEARING . . . I'VE JUST HEARD ENOUGH

It's all my fault. My secret yard sale totally crushed her and still she took me to Little Moose Cove to make me happy. Am I the worst person or what? In a few days, I'll be on a plane heading back to Maryland, leaving a bigger mess than the one in Bea's bedroom. Now that Bea's sick, Mom will be more convinced than ever that my grandmother can't live by herself.

"Earth to Shayne," Poppy says with a mouth full of pepperoni pizza. "Did you hear what I said?"

I take my dinner plate and scrape my leftovers into the trash. "Sorry. I have a lot on my mind."

"Well, sure." Poppy lowers her eyes and plays with the corners of her paper napkin. "But that's why I think we should go out."

"I don't know. I'm kind of tired." That's an understatement. My energy level is somewhere between snail and sloth.

"Come on. You love Lolli's. This could be your last chance to go until next summer." Poppy peeks at her watch.

If there is a next summer.

From Poppy's kitchen window, I can see Linc's tent across the water glowing in the dark from the small lantern he keeps inside. Has he been in there all this time? He thinks I wasn't a true friend, that I blabbed his secret. How can I prove to him that I didn't?

"The only reason you want to go to Lolli's is because all your friends will be there," I say.

"Okay, full disclosure: I didn't tell you, but Gio was the one who called to tell me about it, and I'm kind of excited. But there's another reason, too. You need to be there to field questions about Bea. First she makes a scene at your yard sale and now she collapsed. No offense, but people talk on this island, and if you don't set the record straight early on, then rumors about Bea will spread, true or not. You don't want that to happen, do you?"

She offers a hand and I let her lead me upstairs. Muffled sounds from a television show seep under the door of Leanne's room. Poppy complained to her mother that we were old enough to stay home alone, but Mrs. Quayle, who was running late to her garden club, said Leanne should stay in case I needed a ride to the hospital.

Poppy flings a series of T-shirts out her drawer, and they cascade to the floor like parachutes. She chooses a blue one with a Skittles graphic printed on the front, and then pulls on a pair of white denim shorts with rips down the front. I lie on her bed and use her stuffed unicorn as a pillow. My mind wanders to the call I had with my mom earlier when she told me the doctor said Bea has pneumonia. Dry cough, weakness, confusion, Bea had all the symptoms. Bea thinks she caught a cold that never went away, but Mom has her own theory. She thinks all the clutter in Bea's house and the dampness in the air created a habitat for mold to grow and spread. I guess if you inhale that stuff all the time, it can really make you sick and cause respiratory problems like what Bea has. Mom's flying up tonight but said I should stay with Poppy since she's getting in late.

"Want me to do your makeup?" Poppy asks, interrupting my thoughts. She opens a toolbox full of eye shadows, brushes, lip glosses, and powders.

"Where'd you get all this?" I ask as I unscrew the cap of a silver tube and sniff the contents.

"Leanne gives me her old stuff." She chooses a mint-colored shadow and holds my chin steady with one hand while she sweeps the powder over my eyelid. "So did I tell you that Mona's mad at me?"

"She's always mad at you," I say as a soft brush dusts my cheeks. "What's wrong now?"

"She claims I've been reading her diary, which I have, but I'm not admitting it." Poppy hands me a magnified mirror. "There. You look fabulous!"

I study my new made-up face. Hmmm, I can't tell if green makes me look glam or like I belong on a beanstalk.

"Now, all we need to do is fix your hair and we're good to go."

I hand her back the mirror and curl into the fetal position. "Ugh, I can't go anywhere. Bea's in the hospital and Linc's mad at me. I can't deal with it all. If you want to see your friends, go ahead. I understand."

"Uh-huh," Poppy says as she braids a small section of my hair. "Oooooooh, I have a great idea. We should pierce your ears."

My hands automatically cover my lobes. "Very funny."

"I'm serious, I can do it." She scampers out of the room, and seconds later I hear her opening cabinets and slamming drawers in the bathroom across the hall. When she returns, her arms are full of supplies: rubbing alcohol, cotton balls, a sewing kit, and a small cup of ice.

My eyebrows shoot up. "What are you doing?"

"It's not a big deal." She returns to the bed to tug on my left ear. "Once you ice it, you don't even feel the needle go through."

I push her hand away. "No, thanks."

"Well, I'm bored." She puffs out her lower lip and bounces her finger on the top of the needle, lightly at first, then with more force until a pinprick of blood emerges. She shows me. "Ha. Wanna be blood sisters?"

My reply is a blank stare.

Poppy wipes the blood on the underside of her shirt. "Come on, let me pierce your ears. It will be over in seconds."

"No."

"Maybe this will change your mind." She dives under her bed, surfaces with a tiny white box, and lifts the lid.

My heart lodges in my throat when I see what's inside. A pair of silver dolphin earrings, the same ones she showed me in the Cod Café gift shop.

Poppy douses a cotton ball with the rubbing alcohol and wipes down the needle. "These can be yours if you sit there like a good girl." She reaches for my head.

"Quit it." I bat her hand away. But she won't let up. She grabs my shoulders, and we tumble onto the carpet. The next thing I know, we're in a full-on wrestling match. Somehow she manages to straddle me flat on my back and pin my arms down with her legs.

"That was easy. You're such a weakling," she says.

"*You're* a weakling," I scream back as I twist out from under her.

The needle in her hand brushes my upper arm and I feel a sting. An angry red line threatens to grow into an even bigger welt. I point it out to her. "Look what you did."

She tosses the needle into the cup of ice and crouches into a wrestling stance. "Takedown, two points. Let's go again."

"Leave me alone," I say, but she lunges at me anyway. We roll on the floor, grappling at each other's shoulders, hands, anything to overpower the other. I land on my stomach, and she lies flat on top of me, leaving me nowhere to look but into the blackness under her bed. In that dark, I finally see the light. My longtime friend, my summer sister, doesn't give two cents about me anymore. She doesn't care that I had the worst day of my life. She doesn't care that my grandmother almost died in front of my eyes. All she cares about is what *she* wants to do.

She smacks the ground with her hand. "One . . . two . . . two and a half . . ."

Red, white, and blue swirls come in and out of focus. But it's the glint of copper that snaps me to attention. With a grunt worthy of a tennis pro, I free my arm out from Poppy's weight. Sweeping it under the bed, I feel the pointed edges of a bronzed star.

"Get *off*," I say with the force of a hundred lions. Finally, she lifts herself off of me, and we both scramble to our feet.

My chest heaves. I dangle Linc's medal in front of her face. "Where did you get this?"

Fear flashes in her eyes before she pulls a composed face. "I don't know."

"This is Linc's. Why do you have it?" My mouth is an avalanche. I cannot stop. "And why did you steal those earrings?"

Her eyes darken. "Those are Mona's."

But I can tell from the way her eyes dart around that she's lying. We stand, facing each other, the silence between us charged and dangerous. I feel like the lid on our lobster pot is about to blow.

"Don't lie. Those are the exact earrings you showed me at the gift shop. I'm not stupid. So now you shoplift and you stole Linc's medal."

"I didn't steal his medal. I just found it," she spits.

"Where?" I press.

Her eyes bounce nervously around the room. "It might have been near Cranky's house. I don't remember."

"Give me a break. It fell off Linc's jacket after you clobbered him with a football. I bet you found it right there in the grass, but what I don't understand is why you thought it was okay to take it."

She shakes her head. "You're so obsessed with him, it's embarrassing."

"I'm not obsessed. While you've been judging him up and down, he's actually been a real friend to me."

"Is that why you took him to Little Moose? That was supposed to be our tradition, but I guess you like him better than me."

"Right now I do, because he doesn't take things that aren't his! That medal is not only a family heirloom; it holds special meaning to Linc. And don't tell me you took it because no one pays attention to you, because *I* pay attention. Not that you care."

Poppy's mouth drops wide open. "I don't care? I give you a place to stay while your grandmother's in the hospital and this is the thanks I get? How dare you accuse me? You come here for a few weeks every summer, and I'm supposed to rearrange my whole life to make sure *you* have a good time? Well, guess what? I'm sick of being your camp counselor, and I can't wait for you to go home."

Her words slap me across the face. Part of me wants to cry. But my eyes stay dry. "I'll go home now, if that's what you want."

With clenched fists, Poppy storms out of the room. My body trembles as I pack up my pajamas and toothbrush. I tiptoe down the stairs. The house is quiet as if it's holding its breath. A single lamp illuminates the foyer. On a side table by the front door, I see the blue-and-green friendship bracelet I made for her. Cut in half.

CHAPTER 31

KEEP CALM AND EAT CHOCOLATE

I'm shaking so hard, my teeth chatter. My sneakers shuffle in the damp grass as I follow the path toward Bea's house. Something catches my toe, and I stumble, but the medal remains safe in my clutched hand.

Up ahead, Bea's darkened house and empty driveway tell me that either my mom's plane hasn't landed yet or she went straight to the hospital. I wish she were here.

I make a beeline for Linc's illuminated tent, which shines like a lighthouse in a lonely sea. At least there's one thing I can make right tonight.

"Linc, it's me," I say, knocking on the flaps.

"Go away," he says, his voice muffled by the tent.

I go in anyway. He's lying on his cot, bundled in an army-green sleeping bag.

He sits up on his elbows, his eyes squinty and sleepy. "I said go away, turncoat."

"If I was a turncoat then I wouldn't be bringing you this."

The Medal of Honor's bronze star dangles from my fingers.

Linc snaps to attention and scrambles out of his sleeping bag. "You found it!"

I perch myself at the end of his cot and hand him his treasured medal. He cups it in his hands like a newly hatched chick.

"Where was it?" he asks.

Immediately, I think up things to tell him. That I stumbled upon it as I was walking home or a dog dragged it to the other side of the cove. But I'm tired of watching what I say and covering other people's tracks. So, I do what's right: I tell him the truth.

"Poppy had it in her room."

He sucks in his breath. "That thief! How did she get her hands on it?"

"Remember that day the three of us played catch? After you went inside, Poppy found it, but instead of telling me, she snuck it in her pocket."

Linc shakes his head in disgust.

"Trust me, I'm so mad at her, I may never talk to her again."

He looks up at me. "I didn't mean to call you a turncoat. I was upset."

I nod. "It's okay."

Something distracts him. He scrunches his face. "You're bleeding."

"I am?"

Linc points to blood trickling from the needle scrape above my elbow. He reaches underneath the cot and returns with a plastic first-aid kit. "Always be prepared," he announces before handing me a Band-Aid.

"Thanks," I say as I peel off the protective paper.

"How's Bea? Have you heard anything?" he asks.

"She's fine, but they're going to keep her in the hospital for a couple days. My mom's probably with her now. I'm not sure what time she'll get back here tonight. I really don't want to go into that house alone."

"I know what you mean. My grandpa's not back, either. You can hang out with me for a while. That is . . . if you want to."

"Sure." I hug my knees against my chest. "Thanks."

Linc reaches under his pillow and pulls out a square of blue cloth. He lays the medal on top, lifts the sides of the cloth, and secures it carefully with a safety pin. It's only then that he fully relaxes; a peaceful grin spreads across his face.

My stomach growls like a bear emerging from her winter den, and we both hear it.

"Hungry?" he asks with a laugh.

"I guess. But I don't want that gross cracker thing again."

"Hardtack? Don't worry, I don't have any more, but I do have this." A full-sized chocolate bar appears from inside the first-aid box.

Now it's my turn to laugh. "You definitely are prepared. But, hey, does Hershey's qualify as authentic reenactor food?"

"It does now." He breaks me off a piece.

CHAPTER 32

EVERY FAMILY HAS A STORY

The next afternoon, Cranky drives me and Linc to the hospital since my mom had to leave earlier to meet with Bea's doctor. Bea's still weak and her cough hasn't gone away, but when she sees me, she beckons for me to come close, and she gives me a kiss on the forehead. "I owe you one," she whispers in my ear. Mom says Bea will recover from the pneumonia, but she will need more help to heal her mind. The doctor gave Mom a pamphlet about hoarding. He said when someone really close to you dies, sometimes it can lead to extreme behavior, and maybe Bea also experienced depression or anxiety, which makes hoarding worse. He suggested Bea talk to someone, like a doctor or therapist, to sort out what's bothering her deep inside.

In a weird way, I'm glad Bea got sick at Little Moose. Everything is out in the open now. No more secrets. I have to give my mom credit. When she saw the state of Bea's bedroom, I thought she'd have a complete meltdown. But, instead, she hugged me and we cried together. It wasn't scary, though. It felt more like a sigh of relief, like when the grip of fog lifts and you can see clearly again.

Country music pipes through the speakers of Cranky's pickup truck as he drives us home. It's a little squishy in the front cab for all three of us, so I crack my window open to get some air.

As we cross the bridge that connects the mainland to Cedar Island, I see a homemade sign at the side of the road. BLUE-BERRIES UP AHEAD, it says in black painted letters. Moments later, we pass a man slouched in a director's chair. The opened hatch of his car shades the little cartons of blueberries inside. It reminds me of the flea market and the downward spiral that happened after that. Now that Bea's sick, she'll have more problems on top of problems. Thinking about it makes my head spin.

My nerves feel shaky, so I pull out some embroidery floss from my hip pocket to start a new bracelet. I knot the purple, brown, and white threads at the top and fan them out into a sunbeam on my lap. I've made so many bracelets on this trip. An idea pops in my brain. What if I sold them, like I'd told Linc I would, but it would be a fund-raiser, like the way people sell rubber bracelets to raise money for a good cause.

A fund-raiser for Bea. I like the sound of that.

I nudge Linc. "Hey, what would you think if I went ahead with my bracelet sale but—"

He cuts me off. "You don't need to do that anymore. You found the medal."

"Medal?" Cranky turns down the radio. "You're not still messin' around with that, are you?"

Linc and I glance at each other. I mouth the word *oops* and he grimaces in return.

He takes a deep breath. "Grandpa, I have a confession to make. I did mess around with it. In fact, I lost it for a little while."

Cranky opens his mouth to speak, but Linc stops him. "I was going to tell you, honest, but—happy ending—Shayne found it, and I put it back in your desk where it belongs. Look, I understand if you're mad. You risked your life for it and I should have been more careful. I was irresponsible. I'm really sorry." He hangs his head.

Cranky scrunches his face. "I didn't risk my life for the medal."

"Yes, you did," Linc says. "You ran into the fire."

"Are you crazy? You think I ran into a burning house to save that old thing?"

Linc's face clenches. His hands ball into fists. "I think *you're* crazy!"

"Don't raise your voice at me, boy." Cranky jerks the wheel and the truck lurches as he pulls us off to the shoulder of the road. He kills the ignition and unbuckles his seat belt. The hairs on my arm prickle. What is he going to do?

Cranky reaches around to his back pocket and removes a worn, brown leather wallet. He opens it and pulls out a crinkled picture. "This was what I ran in for."

A thick white border frames the washed-out photo of an older couple hovering over a man with a scraggly beard. In the man's arm is an infant swaddled in a plush blue blanket.

At first, I don't recognize the dark-haired older man who's beaming at the little baby. But then I realize I'm looking at a younger Cranky. It's almost jarring to see him all happy like that. I've never seen him beam, let alone smile, come to think of it.

Cranky sees me staring and points to the blond woman in the picture. "That's my wife, Cathy, and that's my son, Henry," he says of the bearded man. "And that little baby is the guy you're sitting next to."

I marvel at baby Linc's bald round head and squishy cheeks. "Awww, you're so fat and cute."

Linc nods. "I have to agree with you, there."

The corners of Cranky's mouth turn up ever so slightly. "This picture was your grandmother's prized possession. She kept it on her nightstand and would blow you and your dad a kiss before bed every night. I'm glad I was able to save it." He folds the picture back into his wallet. "It's all I've got left. My wife's gone, and you and your dad . . ." He hesitates and starts up the engine. "You don't come around so much anymore."

Linc looks down at his lap. "Maybe we can visit more often. I'll ask my dad when he comes back."

Cranky nods in approval and steers the truck back onto the road. Nobody talks the rest of the way home. When we get to his house, he parks the pickup in the driveway but doesn't get out. Something tells me I should stay put, so the three of us stare straight ahead at the cove in front of us.

"I've made a decision," he suddenly says, gripping the wheel. "I'm not going to give the medal to a museum. I'll keep it here, so you'll have something to look forward to when you come back."

Linc's eyes light up. "Seriously?"

Cranky glances at him. "I'm always serious."

Linc offers him a hand. "Thanks, Grandpa."

They shake on it.

DON'T LOOK BACK...
YOU'RE NOT GOING THAT WAY

THOMAS COVE ~~yard~~ BRACELET SALE! EVERYTHING MUST GO!

Bea's only been out of the hospital for a couple days, but she's already feeling stronger. She seems to love having my mom around. They haven't fought once, which is a miracle. Even when Bea said she wanted to join me at my sale this morning, Mom told her she had to stay home and rest, and Bea actually listened to her. My recycled cardboard sign leans against the metal legs of the folding table. Linc sits on a plastic lawn chair with the empty cashbox in front of him. I arrange and rearrange my bracelets—first grouped by pattern, then color, then pattern again—and wait for a customer. This time we set up our stand on the side of the road near the entrance to Thomas Cove, hoping for more visibility. A car approaches, and I wave the sign over my head to flag it down. It whizzes by.

I sigh. "I have a bad feeling about this. What if nobody stops?"

"They will. Be patient." Linc takes a swig from his canteen, and the water dribbles down his chin. "Look, here comes someone now."

I squint into the morning sun at the person walking toward us. As she gets closer, I recognize her. It's one of the locals I've seen over the years, the lady who always wears a flower crown in her hair, even when it rains.

"What do we have here?" She stops at our table and eyes the bracelets. "These are so pretty! Who is the artist?"

Linc points to me. "She is. Wanna buy a bunch?"

"Linc!" I feel my cheeks warm up.

"Well, how else are you going to raise money for Bea?" he asks.

The yellow petals in the lady's crown flutter in the breeze. "Bea? You don't mean Bea from the Cod Café?"

"Yes. She's my grandmother." My voice falters, but I force myself to stay strong. "She got sick and has a lot of bills to pay. If you buy a bracelet, the money will go toward helping her."

She presses a hand over her heart. "That is so sweet. I'd love to help Bea. Whenever my girlfriends and I meet at the Cod Café, we always ask to sit in Bea's section. She's our favorite waitress." She reaches into her purse and pulls out a five-dollar bill. "I'll take the pink one with the yellow hearts, please."

"Thank you so much," I say as she hands the money to Linc.

Flower-crown lady turns to leave, but something holds her back. She returns her gaze to the remaining bracelets on display.

"Would you like to buy another?" I ask.

"How long are you going to be here?" she asks.

I look at my watch. "A few hours, maybe?"

"Got it." She whips out her smartphone. Her thumbs move fast over the keyboard, and I hear the swishing sound that means a message was sent. "Don't go anywhere. We'll be right back," she calls over her shoulder as she hurries away.

Linc and I look at each other.

"What was that all about? And who's 'we'?" he asks.

I wring my hands together. "I don't know. I'm not doing anything wrong, right? Am I going to get in trouble?"

He leans back in his chair. "I doubt it. But I promise I won't run away this time if you do."

"Ha-ha. Thanks."

Turns out I didn't have to worry at all.

Flower-crown lady had texted her friends about my fund-raiser. And they told their friends. And before I knew it, word spread all over town like melted butter. Most of my bracelets sold within the first hour. Then the funniest thing happened: people started bringing stuff from their homes for me to sell, all in the name of raising money for Bea. Ray showed up with a box of last season's Cod Café sweatshirts; a neighbor from down the street brought ten tennis rackets; and even Gio stopped by to contribute an old guitar. Then something even funnier happened: some of the people who bought Bea's things from my doomed yard sale brought them back. I tucked those items away, knowing that I shouldn't have sold them behind her back in the first place.

Later that afternoon, with almost everything sold, I decide to call it a day. Linc and I quickly box the few remaining items from our roadside stand. I'm about to fold up my cardboard sign when one last customer stops by.

Poppy.

She looks like she rolled out of bed in her rumpled gray sweatpants and navy hoodie. An unfortunate acne outbreak speckles her normally smooth forehead.

Linc avoids eye contact with her. "Do you need me for anything else?" he asks. I can tell he's itching to leave.

"No, I'm good, thanks for your help." I hold up my palm and he slaps me a high five.

As Poppy and I face each other, I swallow away the thickness in my throat. After our wicked fight the other night, I thought we'd never speak to each other again, and now that she's standing in front of me, I don't know what to say. Her words still sting, and I'm not sure I'm ready to make up.

She gnaws on her thumbnail and stares at the tin box overflowing with ones, fives, tens, and twenties.

"Make a lot of money?" she asks.

I peer inside. "I hope so." I haven't counted it yet, but in my mental calculations, I've banked at least a few hundred dollars.

Poppy nods. "Looks like there's nothing much left to sell."

"Except for this broken toaster." I hold it up. "Interested? I've also got a couple of bracelets left."

"Really? I . . . uh . . ." Air blows out her lips. "I could use a bracelet. Mine broke."

My eyes narrow.

I pull the two remaining friendship bracelets out of a Ziploc bag. "All I have is rainbow and blue-and-purple stripes."

"Blue and purple, please."

I hand it to her, and in exchange, she gives me a twenty-dollar bill.

"Keep the change."

My nose crinkles. "Are you sure?"

"Well, this is all for Bea, right? Consider it a donation."

"Gosh, thanks." I add her twenty to the cashbox.

She sniffs as her eyes drop. "I thought you'd want to know, I gave the earrings back."

My eyes widen. "You did?"

"Leanne heard us fighting that night, and she went straight to my dad. I've never seen him so mad. He marched me to the Cod Café and made me apologize in front of everybody."

"Wow."

"It was so humiliating. Ray's not going to press charges, but my parents still grounded me for the rest of the summer."

With my finger, I trace a figure eight on the checkered tablecloth. "That sucks."

"Totally." Poppy rubs her nose with the back of her sleeve and blinks to hold back the tears. "I want you to know I wasn't going to do anything with the medal, I swear."

"You can't go around stealing things."

"I know that," she snaps. "I was jealous. You two seemed to be together all the time, having fun without me."

I throw up my hands. "You were never around, and when you were, you always acted like you wanted to be with someone else."

She looks at me briefly before her eyes slip back to the ground. "You're not perfect, either. You worked on Cranky's boat and never told me."

That stops me in my tracks. "You knew?"

She meets my gaze and raises an eyebrow. "I told you people talk."

"Well, it was no secret you hated the guy, and I figured you'd make fun of me."

"So, I can't tease you anymore, is that it? Man, you've changed."

Poppy tries to laugh like it's a joke, but her voice trails off when she sees I'm not amused.

Awkward silence hangs in the air between us.

"So . . . you're leaving tomorrow, huh," she finally says.

"Yep."

"Cool. I mean it's not cool that you're leaving, I just . . ." Her cheeks redden as her voice trails off again. "I wanted to give you something before you left."

She opens a fist to reveal a triangular piece of mint-colored sea glass with a dip in the middle that makes it almost look like a heart. "I thought maybe for Shoppy, or at least something to remember me by."

She explodes into tears. Longtime friends often know what the other's thinking, and this time I'm positive we're both thinking the same thing: our friendship has hit a major wall.

My eyes well up. I reach for her arm. "Look, I'm sorry. I should have told you about Cranky."

She hiccups. "I'm sorry, too. About everything."

We lean across the table to hug, but it's loose and tentative, not the tight squeezes we used to do. I mean, she'll always be a part of Thomas Cove, but I have to stop relying on her to make or break my summer. I spent so much time and energy trying to recreate the memory of us, but being stuck in the past only made us both miserable. It's pretty ironic. We've all tried to stop Bea from hanging on to her things. I guess I need to stop hanging on so tightly, too.

The truth is that both of us have changed. I don't know if we'll ever be friends the exact same way we used to be, but no matter what happens with Poppy, I will always have amazing memories: swims in the cove, searching for sea glass, gorging on lobster rolls—the stuff that's worth remembering.

CHAPTER 34

IN HIGH OR LOW TIDE, I'LL BE BY YOUR SIDE

Back at the house, Mom and Bea sit at the kitchen table while Cranky stands over a bubbling pot on the stove. Ever since Bea's return home, Cranky has doted on her like a mother hen.

"How'd your sale go?" My mom rubs the back of her neck while stretching it from side to side. I know she doesn't like sleeping on the couch, but amazingly she hasn't complained. It's funny how it only took a couple days for her New England accent to creep back in, especially when she talks with Bea about old times and old friends.

Bea adjusts the white cotton blanket draped across her lap and pats my hand. "Tell me everything. Don't leave out any details."

A buzzer goes off, and Cranky removes a batch of muffins from the oven. Streaks of flour cover his black T-shirt. I cover my mouth to hide the giggles.

"Cut me some slack, Lobster Bait. Someone's got to keep the food flowing around here. I've got a bunch of fat lobsters in the fridge and corn on the cob that needs shucking. So, make yourself useful." He plunks a pile of ears on the table.

I pull out a chair and settle in to my shucking station. My mom ties her shoulder-length chestnut hair into a short pony-tail before she takes a few ears; together we peel away layers of green husks to get to the golden kernels underneath.

"I think the whole town showed up," I tell Bea. "Even Ray bought five bracelets."

"Psshh," Bea says, "he's trying to get on my good side. Knowing him, he probably wants me back at the lunch shift tomorrow."

"Oh, that reminds me." I retrieve the wad of money from my pocket and slide it across the table in front of Bea.

She looks bewildered. "What's this?"

"I made three hundred and fifty dollars. It's for you," I say.

My mom's eyes shine with pride, but Bea's not smiling at all. Suddenly, I feel like a shell-less hermit crab, naked and without protection.

Bea sighs. "Honey, your heart is so big, but I can't accept this money."

"You have to," I say, sounding desperate. "This was a fund-raiser for you. Please! I know it's not a lot, but you can use it to pay a bill or something. You don't understand. She's going to make you sell the house."

Bea frowns at my mother. "Over my dead body."

Mom holds up her hands. "Wait a minute, wait a minute. Everybody calm down. Shayne, Bea and I have had a long talk. It's been hard on everybody with Grandpa gone, and maybe I expected too much too soon. But Bea understands that she can't keep living this way and is going to have to make some serious changes."

"You're not selling the pheasant," says Bea.

My mom looks to the ceiling. "I didn't say we were. Anyway . . ." She takes a deep breath before continuing. "Bea's going to come home with us for a little while. It's not permanent, but for now it's not healthy or safe for her to stay here. I also have a friend I want Bea to meet, someone she can talk to."

"Like a therapist?" I cut in.

Bea sits up straight and her jaw tightens for a few seconds before she looks me in the eye. "Yes."

"What will happen with the house?" I ask.

My mom surveys all the piles around us, the clutter, Junk Mountain as tall as ever. She bites her lip. "Nothing for now. When Bea's ready to return home, we'll hire a professional cleaning crew to help us sort it out."

Bea closes her eyes, stressed. "I don't know if I can do this."

My mom squeezes her hand. "It's going to be okay. Bea?

Mom, listen to me. We'll go slowly, I promise. We'll be with you every step of the way."

Bea breathes through her nose until the panic subsides. She opens her eyes and focuses on the wad of money I placed in front of her. She picks it up and weighs it in her palm as if it were a scale. "Shayne, you did good today. I'll take the money, even though you're the one who really deserves it." She tips her head toward Cranky. "Working on his boat for free all this time."

Cranky hands her some pills and a glass of apple juice. "Whatever you say, darlin'."

Bea blushes and takes a sip.

Mom and I exchange bug eyes. *Darling?*

☆

Later in my room, I pack up my suitcase with some of the things I've collected from my stay: the Civil War bullets, some sea glass, even the *Welcome to the Nut House* sign Bea gave me. Out of habit, part of me still wonders if Poppy will show up to say good-bye. We used to stage these big, dramatic departures. We'd hug and pretend to wail, and when my car pulled away, she would run after it like a madwoman. I can't imagine that happening this time.

There's a knock at the door. "Come in," I say.

It's Linc, dressed in full reenactor regalia. His eyes scan

every inch of the room as he steps inside hesitantly, like he's time-traveled into the twenty-first century. He extends his arm, offering me a little package wrapped in a familiar blue cloth. "I brought you a good-bye present."

I throw him a funny look before taking his gift and removing the safety pin at the top. My heart practically stops when I see his great-great-great-grandfather's Medal of Honor in the palm of my hand.

"You . . . You're . . ." I stammer. "You're giving this to me? Wait, what?"

The corners of his mouth turn up. "Well . . . it's not real, if that's what you think."

"Oh." I bust out laughing, part embarrassed, part relieved.

"It's that fake one from the Soldier & Saber. Grandpa and I went there again last night, and when I saw it, I knew I had to buy it for you."

I scrunch my face. "Why?"

"Because you deserve it. You saved Bea's life. You're a hero."

"I don't know about that," I say shyly.

"You were like a colonel out there. If I ever went into battle, I would definitely want you with me. You're the bravest of the brave."

"You were brave, too," I say. "If I was a colonel, then you were like . . . a general."

He shakes his head furiously. "No, NO! General ranks higher than a colonel."

"Then, you were like a sergeant."

He looks disappointed. "That low?"

I grab his shoulders and give him a gentle shake. "How about we both did a good job?"

He stuffs his hands in the front of his coat pockets and rocks on his heels. "Okay."

I rub the smooth ribbon of the fake medal between my fingers. I used to think the best thing about Thomas Cove was that nothing ever changes, but I don't think that anymore. Like Linc said, sometimes change can surprise you in a good way.

"So . . . see you next summer?" Linc's voice is full of hope.

I don't hesitate to answer. "Yes. Definitely."

I unzip the small front pocket on my suitcase and dig out a bracelet, the first one I made when I got here. The pattern's a little uneven, but the colors are perfect. Blue and gray. The colors of Cranky's lobster buoys. The Union and Confederacy living in harmony. I offer it to Linc. "You don't have to wear it, but . . . something to remember me by."

He gives a sheepish grin and sticks out his arm.

I tie the bracelet around his wrist.

ACKNOWLEDGMENTS

Thank you to Deborah Vetter for your tutelage during first drafts; Lisa Tillman for your great input over many revisions and cups of coffee; Amy Jameson for being an awesome agent and support system; Adrienne Szpyrka for being a wonderful, caring editor; Teresa Bonaddio for creating a beautiful cover; and finally, my family for letting me drag you along fact-finding missions up and down Mid-Coast Maine for many years.

ABOUT THE AUTHOR

Lauren Abbey Greenberg is an award-winning writer/ producer and a graduate of the Institute of Children's Literature. She lives in Maryland with her husband, two children, and fluffy dog, and has spent summers in Maine for the past twenty years. This is her debut novel. Visit her online at www.laurenabbeygreenberg.com.